Stops Along the Way

Also by Anna Sortino

Give Me a Sign

On the Bright Side

Stops Along the Way

ANNA SORTINO

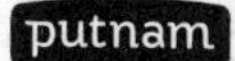

G. P. Putnam's Sons

G. P. Putnam's Sons
An imprint of Penguin Random House LLC
1745 Broadway, New York, NY 10019
penguinrandomhouse.com

Design by Nicole Rheingans
Text set in FF Milo Serif

Library of Congress Cataloging-in-Publication Data
Names: Sortino, Anna author
Title: Stops along the way / Anna Sortino.
Description: New York: G. P. Putnam's Sons, 2026.
Summary: A road trip with her sister, who has a rare genetic disease that Iris may also inherit, and Declan, her board game rival–turned–travel companion, forces cautious, deaf Iris to face the fear of going blind, navigate family tensions and unexpected detours, and confront the surprising odds of falling in love.
Identifiers: LCCN 2025038445 (print) | LCCN 2025038446 (ebook)
ISBN 9798217005178 hardcover | ISBN 9798217005185 epub
Subjects: CYAC: Sisters—Fiction | Automobile travel—Fiction
Deaf people—Fiction | Blind people—Fiction
People with disabilities—Fiction | Romance stories
LCGFT: Romance fiction | Novels
Classification: LCC PZ7.1.S6796 St 2026 (print) | LCC PZ7.1.S6796 (ebook)
LC record available at https://lccn.loc.gov/2025038445
LC ebook record available at https://lccn.loc.gov/2025038446

First published in the United States of America by G. P. Putnam's Sons, 2026

Manufactured in the United States of America
LSCC

ISBN 9798217005178
1st Printing

The authorized representative in the EU for product safety and compliance is Penguin Random House Ireland, Morrison Chambers, 32 Nassau Street, Dublin D02 YH68, Ireland, https://eu-contact.penguin.ie.

Stops Along the Way

Chapter One

It's a one-mile walk to the strip mall that houses Roll Again Games. Not the pleasant kind of walk, either, but a journey down the sidewalk of a road that has four lanes of traffic with drivers all going at least ten miles over the speed limit in each direction. I should tie back my long blond hair, but the strong gusts of wind make a quick mess of it no matter what I do, so right now it's swirling around my head like my own personal tornado.

I'm trying to play Taylor Swift's latest album, but the Bluetooth keeps disconnecting from my hearing aids, which makes for a staticky and frustrating listening experience. It finally manages to connect long enough to reach a fantastic bridge when an incoming call interrupts and rings loudly directly into my ears.

It's my sister, of course. I answer the call. Who else would I actually talk to on the phone?

Like always, it's bad timing. We've been playing phone tag for nearly a year now since she left for college.

"Hey, Lee—" I start, but Amelia launches right into something I can't hear over the noise. "What was that?" I shout at my cell phone. She's still rambling on. "Wait, I have not heard a single word you've said."

There's a lull in traffic as I near the stoplight intersection where I need to cross the street. There's a family walking their dog in the opposite direction. I nod toward them as I advance to the other side of the road.

"Where are you?" Amelia asks. "I'm just trying to figure some stuff out real quick. How much do you actually need the car this summer?"

I laugh, uninhibited and wild, at the absurdity of what she's saying to me right now. A driver stuck at the light glances my way. "You're asking me this as I'm *literally* walking on the side of the highway."

"It's not a highway." She's quick to correct, assuming where I am. "It's just a road."

"I'm not debating the definition of a highway with you right now as I'm walking next to one. Yes, I need the car."

"On your way to game night, right? You're still doing that?"

I roll my eyes and adjust the strap of my bag that's been digging into my shoulder. "Yes, I told you about the new character drop. I got the Fortune Teller, who has action cards that—"

"I think I've just outgrown playing Rivalry," she continues, stuck on her own thought, asking me another question without listening to my answer. "Doesn't Peyton drive you sometimes?"

We're often on a similar wavelength that enables conversational shortcuts, but sometimes it just feels like I'm being steamrolled. "She has to watch her brothers tonight."

Amelia is speaking again, but quieter now—and not to me, I realize. It seems like she's dropped the phone away from her ear to talk to someone else, probably her roommate.

My sister is only a year older than me—and still many, many years younger than several of the people I'll see at Roll Again Games in a few minutes—but since she went off to college, she's been abandoning our shared hobbies, like this board game, Rivalry, that we used to play all weekend long, imagining elaborate backstories for our chosen character decks. We didn't even fully understand the game's rules back then. We'd just roll dice and swap cards at random until we eventually declared a winner.

(Which meant that, as the older sibling, Amelia usually "won.")

We've been growing apart for a while now, but the roots took hold long before she even left for school in Philadelphia. If I had to pinpoint an exact moment where I finally stumbled upon a divide between the two of us, it would be Amelia's diagnosis.

These days it still isn't obvious to most people. Put us in front of any stranger and ask them to spot the difference, and they likely wouldn't discover how we no longer experience the world the same way. However, I've felt the wedge driven between us, even if it goes unaddressed for the most part.

Five years ago, when Amelia started high school, she began having difficulty reading the board, which led to several doctors' appointments. Eventually, she got diagnosed with a rare eye disease that causes central vision loss. Our parents shed tears that they tried and failed to keep secret from us, but somehow Amelia kept her chin up, almost unfazed.

I know my sister better than to buy into that act.

I know why she gave up playing Rivalry with me. Her growing frustration at not being able to take in the entire game board the way she once did, each turn taking just a bit longer for her to get her bearings. The effort to play outmatching her enthusiasm for the game until, ultimately, she insisted she simply wasn't interested.

Eager to keep my favorite opponent, I researched and found a large-print edition, but by then, I wasn't sure how to push her about it. I wasn't going to beg. Instead, the large-print box sits on a shelf in the family room, collecting dust, along with our original Red Witch and Twilight Elf character kits.

"I'm almost there. Hello? Lee," I say, dragging out the *ee* of her name until she returns her focus to our call, wrapping up whatever she was discussing with her roommate.

"Sorry, yeah, so okay, I was thinking—" Amelia says right as the Bluetooth cuts out again and the call drops. She doesn't hesitate to call back and continue talking as if we were never disconnected. "What I'm trying to figure out is how exactly I'm getting the car home for the summer."

I step carefully over an uneven sidewalk crack. The obvious comes to mind. "By driving it?"

It's easy to picture her lying on her dorm room bed, pursing her lips together and humming for a moment before she raises her concern with that plan. "It's at least eighteen hours from Philly back to Omaha. More like twenty-plus, with traffic and stops."

"I remember." From having driven all that way with our parents last fall to drop her off at school.

She ignores the snark in my voice. "How am I supposed to drive it back by myself now?"

"I don't know? Do you have any friends who need a ride in this direction?"

"Well, Mom said maybe—"

"I just got here, and I'm a little late, so we can figure it out later." I hold my bag level, trying to keep the box inside upright. I pick up my pace as the path veers right into a small strip mall with a nail salon, dollar store, Chinese takeout counter, and my beloved board game shop, Roll Again Games. This walk always takes me longer than I expect it to.

"Sure. I don't call you enough," Amelia teases, "but when I do, you have to go?"

"You call me when I'm running late to Rivalry!"

"You call me when I'm in class!"

"Who takes a night class?"

"It was the only section of Social Media and Society that was offered this semester."

"That's not my fault." I hop off the sidewalk to save a few seconds cutting across the small parking lot, empty except for a few vehicles parked in front of the shops, but have to jump onto the curb when a stealthily silent car sneaks up behind me. "Ah! I almost died."

"What?" Amelia is quick to ask.

"Miss you, bye!" I say, hanging up the phone as I push open the heavy glass door to Roll Again, the bell chiming loudly and alerting everyone to my late arrival while my phone buzzes with a text from my sister.

Amelia: You're not dead, right?

Iris: All good

Amelia: Miss you too!

The shop is cozy, with overhead lamps placed strategically to encourage this mood. I weave around the front displays and low shelves that showcase the newest board game releases, imagining my own creation one day sitting among them. A long shot, but something that inches closer to possible if I place at the Omaha Board Game Expo next month.

I walk along the wall full of used games for resale until I make it around back to the play tables. My bag slips from my shoulder, tilting the box I've been carrying, making a mess of all the pieces inside.

Great.

The store owner, Bryce, waves me to the tables, where the usual crowd is already situated, game decks in hand, waiting for player assignments. He's in his late thirties and wearing an oversized band tee atop a striped long-sleeved shirt. His glasses have slid to the edge of his nose as he stares me down.

"Don't worry, Iris. I've already got your name queued up." Bryce taps on the random generator app on his tablet as I slink into a seat at the empty folding card table in the back. "Shit, it just rebooted. It'll only be a few more seconds."

Sally, a cheery woman in her sixties and self-proclaimed gamer grandma, turns around to offer me a platter of homemade cookies. I smile a thank-you and grab one, nodding apologetically as she also presses a napkin into my hand. I know better, especially after Declan's smudgy fingers nearly stuck a chocolate fingerprint on my precious character art last month.

Is Declan here? I don't see him.

Christopher and Lucas—the father-son duo who is very serious about consulting the rule book—are next to me, and a couple of the other teens my age are up front, but there's no Declan in sight, which is probably for the best, because I keep getting stuck playing against him lately.

Some random generator that is.

Although I guess we are both here the most often.

I pull my game deck out of my bag and place it on the table in front of me. As expected, the cover of the cardboard box has slid up half an inch, which is all it took for the pieces inside to dislodge from their places. I should buy a travel kit, but the affordable option would be a boring black case, whereas this box has a gorgeous blue-and-gray-tone illustration of the

Fortune Teller on the cover. Sure, the corners might be getting a little worse for wear, but that just shows how much I love this set.

The reflective shine on the Fortune Teller's crystal ball. Her wavy gown and chin held high. Her long gray hair. And her sparkling gray eyes, clouded, mysterious, and not particularly focused—suggesting that, while she can see multiple futures, her own vision isn't clear.

I'm well aware that blind eyes aren't always so obvious.

"All right," Bryce says, holding up his tablet and quieting all the side conversations. "We're up and running. Tonight it'll be Sally versus Leslie. Christopher versus Mischa. Dakota versus Shakir. Roy versus Lucas." That seems to be everyone . . . except me. Wait, we have an odd number tonight? "And Iris versus Declan."

Again? I'm not surprised, but I am confused.

While the others stand from where they've been sitting, shuffling around to new tables to face off against their opponents, I walk over to Bryce. "Um, I don't think Declan is here."

"Oh, he's sorting some stock for me. You can go grab him."

"He works here now?"

"A couple hours when I can use the help," Bryce says, still fidgeting with the tablet.

In the back, there's a closet-sized storage room where Bryce shoves all incoming restock shipments. The door is ajar, and I find Declan standing next to a stack of cardboard boxes, with the one on top flapped open, revealing all the dice packets that will be added to the display shelf, but he seems to have been halted mid-task with a somewhat intense phone call.

One that I'm uncomfortable interrupting.

I've never seen Declan "The Dice Love Me" Weber look so serious. Although I do see him almost every single week in that same yellow hoodie with a single stripe across the chest, like some unofficial game-night uniform he always dons. It's either that or the matching green one. I should start flipping a coin to guess what outfit he'll show up in each week.

Declan glances in my direction, and his hunched shoulders relax as if he's pretending he was unbothered the whole time. He turns around, voice lowered so that I can't hear his parting words as he hangs up the phone, before facing me again.

"Game time?" He arches an eyebrow. "You again?"

"*You* again?" I cross my arms. I can never get a read on this guy.

"Some random generator," Declan mumbles.

"I was *just* thinking that."

He trails behind me back to our table, grabbing his Space Pirate—the cliché dude character of choice—deck from the front counter. "I hope you're feeling confident, because I can already tell the dice are going to love me tonight."

"If you say that every night, you can't possibly be right."

"The more often I say it, the more times it'll be right."

I smirk. "Sure, because that's how it works . . ."

The first thing Declan removes from his character box is a slim little softcover notebook, where he's logged all his match stats, and he flips it open past the other competitors to a page with my name at the top. I crane my neck to read it, and he's all too eager to hold it up for me to get a better view.

I scrunch my nose at the shortage of tallies in my column of overall wins compared to his. He's got a clear lead over me.

This boy loves a spreadsheet. He's also broken these stats down even further to indicate how many times various gameplay situations have been enacted, such as when a player has gotten to use their character's full power—a somewhat rare Yahtzee-style move when the designated character number is rolled from all the dice.

Threes for his Space Pirate. Ones for my Fortune Teller.

Declan sets his notebook aside and shuffles his action cards, bending them in the center as he does so, like he's preparing for a poker match. I'm much more careful, sliding them side to side, not wanting to jeopardize the character art.

With our dice and tokens also displayed before us, we're finally ready to start our match.

My hearing aids don't usually pick up much background noise, but here, when there's multiple games going on at once, I love that I'm clued in to the sounds of clattering dice and cards slicking off the tops of decks.

We each roll a die to see who will play first, and I get the higher number.

Then I start by drawing an action card. Declan makes a mark in his notebook, which makes my teeth clench. "Are you going to do that for every single move?"

He nods, not looking up at me. "Well, a while ago, you made some dig about winning more often than me . . . which, as we can see"—he gestures to the page in front of him—"the numbers clearly dispute."

"That total can't be right," I protest.

"You should've kept your own record. But you claimed you were winning because you actually *strategize*. Which is why I started keeping track of how often you led with an action or a roll, and whether it was successful. I got to say, you're getting really predictable."

"So are you, *Yellow*."

"Yellow?" He tilts his head and glances down at the cards on the table, not realizing my comment is on his attire.

"It's your turn; roll the freaking dice already."

Which he does, starting off with an initial attack that my action card only partially thwarts. I groan and lower my cardboard health-status dial. Declan makes yet another mark in his notebook.

"Just noting my opening success," he explains. "In order to calculate the probability and such."

I roll my own dice, with a less fruitful yield, but one that at least hits him with three points of damage in conjunction with my aforementioned action card. It's all about future planning.

"I'm decidedly not a fan of probability," I admit.

My mind drifts to *genetic* probability, but I do my best to not think about that, even though those odds are never far from my mind. Right now I can't be distracted against a formidable opponent, one who plays the game as if nothing can touch him.

"You've got to take a deep breath." Declan exhales for show. "And go along for the ride. Make the best of wherever the dice take you."

"I'm not the one who should be rethinking their strategy."

He laughs. "The numbers disagree."

Yet his Space Pirate has an unsuccessful roll, an attack that my Fortune Teller can easily defend against without any damage. Then, on my turn, I leverage another action card to enhance the strength of future rolls, once again playing the long game.

I'm eager for this to be one of those nights where Declan puts too much faith in some perceived rolling advantage and fails miserably, but the dice really do seem to favor him, and tonight is no exception.

For the next hour, we continue back and forth, launching attacks, mounting defenses, playing special character tricks and other effects, and—I'll reluctantly admit—having a good time.

Declan's easy to be around, even if he frustrates me with every little tally he adds to that obnoxious notebook.

It's only a matter of time until one of our characters' health statuses drops to zero, concluding tonight's battle. It's strange to see health conceptualized as simply as that, but I'd be lying if I said I wasn't giddy watching Declan's number continue to fall.

My next roll is a decent attack, so maybe, just maybe, I've got a chance of winning this thing.

He senses that too. "The dice must be feeling sympathetic to you," he admits, reducing the cardboard tracker by another three points, putting him at a dangerously low number that he might not manage to recover from. "At least I'm still hanging on."

"Your love of numbers feels at odds with how much you're willing to trust the dice."

"I'm happy being a contradiction. Keeps you on your toes."

"Not for long." I slap down my latest action card, which gives me the opportunity to double my next attack and put him out of his misery. If . . . my next roll allows the ability.

I toss my blue-and-gray dice onto the table and fixate on each disappointing bounce. Nope, nope, nope.

Declan clings to his momentary success, throwing his six red-and-gold dice out with a flourish, his eyes widening as each turns over to reveal a perfect set of matching threes.

He sits there, silent.

I jump up from my chair, shaking my head furiously, and my ponytail slaps me in the face. "Did you sell your soul to these dice or what?"

Declan is still staring at the table with utter amazement. On the first throw. With no card-manipulation effects or anything. He achieved a Hail Mary roll that activates his Space Pirate's most powerful attack, dealing me undefendable damage that wins him what, ten seconds ago, was an unwinnable game.

I didn't notice that two tables have already cleared and gone home for the night, but the others still here get up to look at what's happened. Roy claps Declan on the back, congratulating him on his luck.

Declan casually nudges his attack token in my direction. Calculating the damage, I lower my health status to negative three before tossing the cardboard tracker back onto the table and slumping into my seat. "I want a rematch."

He doesn't start packing up his game yet, leaving the victorious threes between us. "I'm sure that'll happen soon enough."

"Well, there's just this summer, because then I'm off to Indianapolis, where I finally get to find someone else to play against."

He looks up from adding more stats to his notebook and squints at me. "You're going to college in Indy?"

I lean back, tilting up my chin defensively. "Yeah?"

I applied to a couple different schools, including here in Nebraska, but ended up choosing to cross the Midwest, especially after getting a solid scholarship. I'm not going quite as far from Omaha as Amelia did, but I wanted to stray away from home too.

Declan runs a hand through his dark hair. ". . . Go Dawgs?"

My face drops. "Stop."

He chuckles, shaking his head as he makes a dramatic showing of adding another tally to his overall-wins column. "Oh, man, Butler doesn't know what's coming."

We're going to the same college this fall? We don't even go to the same high school right now. It's not that big of a university. Seriously, what are the odds?

Freaking probability.

I push my palms down on the table to stand, quickly packing my game components back into the box and sending a text to my parents asking if one of them can come pick me up.

"Guess I'll be stuck playing with you and your ridiculous dice. Hopefully, their board game club has a bigger pool of people so we don't have to play each other as often."

Declan smiles. "Do you want a fresh page, or should I just continue our current stats, seeing as I'm already in the overall lead?"

I bite my lip. "I don't care about your notebook," I lie.

On my way out the door, Bryce calls out from behind the counter. "Hey, don't forget we've got a couple upcoming playthroughs on the calendar to test all your guys' contest entries before the expo. How's your game coming along?"

"I've got everything all outlined," I say. "But I'll have to wait until after finals next week to put the actual cards and design together. How professional does it need to look to stand a chance?"

"Don't worry, the judges really do favor concept over polish. There was some dude last year who spent thousands of dollars dressing up his terrible Settlers of Catan–knockoff concept, and then it didn't place at all. Just be as creative as you can be and not, like, messy, and you'll be good."

I didn't realize Declan had walked up beside me. "Did you ever show me what you've been working on?" he asks.

"No, but I'll tell you one thing." I give a pointed smile. "It doesn't include dice."

Chapter Two

My orange graduation cap slips down my head as I round the stage. I do a clumsy job readjusting it for the posed photographer before offering an enthusiastic smile to the crowd, where my family is sitting somewhere I can't locate with their cameras presumably also trained in my direction.

I follow the line of students ahead of me, weaving our way through the aisles, to sit back down in my folding chair in the front. Peyton plops down in hers first. She's wearing sneakers, jeans, and a light sweater vest beneath her gown, much comfier than this ridiculous dress I'm wearing, which is riding up in ways I can't adjust right now.

"Loving the bold lip," I say to Peyton. The bright orange suits her dark complexion and matches our gowns in a display of school spirit that she usually reviles.

She leans to whisper something in my ear.

I sit back so I can read her lips. "What was that?"

"My mom wasn't so sure, but even she couldn't discount how good this looks," she repeats at normal volume. Most of our classmates around us have also started chatting. This is going to be a long ceremony. There are rows and rows and rows of students left to go. "How much longer do you think this is going to take?"

The two of us have been favored by alphabetical order throughout our educational career.

Peyton Beckett and Iris Biagi.

"Such is our burden to bear as *the bees*," I joke, pulling out the nickname we gave ourselves all the way back in kindergarten, perhaps invoking it for the last time. Now I'm really feeling sentimental. "Oh, look." I point to the stage.

We both lean our heads together and smile as one of our classmates turns around and takes a selfie with the whole crowd.

"I hope we only have to do that once. Wait, actually . . ." Peyton pulls out her own phone from beneath her robe.

I panic for a second. "We're not supposed to have our phones."

"How many times do I have to tell you? Learn to go with the flow, B," Peyton says as we lean in together for our own photo. I glance around and realize several other people have their phones out as well. "What are they going to do? Take away our diplomas?"

"You didn't know these are notoriously empty?" I flip open the school-engraved cardstock holder. "Until final grades and all that."

Peyton shakes her head. "If they withhold your diploma, I'll forge you a new one."

I laugh. "Putting those graphic design skills to use from day one."

"I'll include it on my résumé."

We sit silently for a few called names as the squeaking of folding chairs grows more and more distant while the rows behind us shuffle through, but they're still only finishing up the *C*'s. With over five hundred students, this is going to take ages. It's getting really warm in this gown.

"Are you still working on your board game?" Peyton asks me.

"Yeah, I finally got it all retooled, but I'm mourning what could have been. Who knew there were already so many games about ancient Rome?"

"Every nerd ever. What'd you end up switching it all to?"

"The Salem witch trials. It's sort of Mafia-slash-Werewolf meets Carcassonne."

She attempts to smooth out the wrinkles in her gown. "I'm not clear on how you're blending those together. Then again, I'm a player, not a creator."

"You sure you don't want to submit something?"

"I play to relax, and trying to come up with my own board game sounds like the opposite of relaxing. Plus, I don't have much spare time. You're picking up shifts again this summer, right?"

"Of course." Her family's restaurant is the only part-time job I ever want to work.

Peyton and I turn forward and make silly faces at our friend Elizabeth Elford, the *E*'s to our *B*'s. She does a cute little wave while keeping her arms down at her sides, nervously crossing the stage, her carefully curled hair sticking out from under the graduation cap and bouncing off the back of her gown.

"What graduation party should we get to first tonight?" I ask Peyton. There are tons of parties spread out throughout the summer, but a few are competing for attendance later today. "I didn't really know Stephanie that well, but apparently, her family goes all out."

Peyton points out a finger for emphasis. "It's a question of do we want to start there *or* end up there."

"Exactly."

"Hmm. I don't know. We can see what Elizabeth wants to do. It doesn't really matter to me, because the best party is in a few weeks." Peyton gestures to herself, as if I didn't already know. "The best people, and the *best* food. No promises about music, though, since my brother wants to DJ."

Her skepticism is understandable. Her brother is eight.

"I can't wait. It'll be my light at the end of the tunnel after submitting this board game and taking an unexpected round trip to Pennsylvania."

Peyton narrows her eyes. "You're visiting your sister?"

"I didn't tell you? We've got to get Amelia's car back here from Pennsylvania. My mom floated the idea of flying me out there so I can drive it back with her."

My sister isn't in attendance at my ceremony since she has her own finals next week. I insisted it wasn't a big deal because these graduation things are long and boring, yet today, especially earlier, gathered with my parents and grandparents, it feels weird for Amelia to not be here too.

Like I was there for her graduation.

Sometimes it's hard not to feel like every aspect of my life is just a follow-up act and that time spent with my sister is entirely at her mercy.

"That is a long trip." Then Peyton does a silly little dance with her hands as she says in a singsong voice, "But then you'll have the *car*."

"A necessity," I agree. My last summer before college, and finally the freedom to drive anywhere I need to go. I join in her dance. "Then I'll have the *car*."

Chapter Three

No matter how hard I try, this budget board game production is going to look like a child's school project stuffed inside a shoebox. Because even as I painstakingly Mod Podge the designs I printed on glossy paper at the library onto this cardboard container, I know there's no hope of this looking like one of the ultra-professional, polished submissions.

I'll just have to hope my concept is solid enough.

The overall winning board games selected from the individual and team submission categories will get produced by a local publisher, with small cash prizes for the runners-up. Money would obviously be great, but seeing my own creation produced, looking all bright and shiny like a *real* board game, would be something else.

I've spent all of this Sunday morning glueing the tile pieces onto reinforced cardstock and cutting each out into identical hexagons with a knife when Amelia calls. I nudge my phone screen with the back of my knuckle to answer.

"Did you check in for your flight?" my sister asks.

"Oh, shoot, not yet." I glance down at the mess of cardboard and glue in front of me. "Can you do it for me? I'm trying to get this all put together so I can submit it early before I leave."

There's loud keyboard clacking streamed through my hearing aids as Amelia jumps into the task. "Sure, is your password still the—"

"Yeah, should be that same one. Maybe add an exclamation mark or two on the end."

I cuss beneath my breath, having started to work too hastily and cut the corner of one piece too short. Setting down the knife, I take stock of all the pieces I still have left to cut out. Is it really worth rushing to finish this before flying out to Amelia?

Then again, I have the momentum now, and the vision for this project in mind. I'll only be more stressed if I put this off for later when I'll end up with less time to finish everything. It's just these connecting board pieces—the town square, courthouse, cottages, woods, and lake tiles—that I need to get this crafty with. The deck portion, with the accusation and enchantment cards I ordered through a photo printing website, should be delivered this afternoon, *just* in time for me to take all these components to the first playthrough scheduled at Roll Again tonight. It will be good to make sure the whole game isn't a mess before I leave it in the submission pile that Bryce has offered to bring over to the expo for us on early registration day.

Admittedly, I'm approaching this the way I did all my homework assignments throughout high school and middle school. I never understood when my classmates would take time to revise a paper over and over again. How much better could it really get? There's such sweet relief in just submitting and being done with something.

The judges are either going to like the concept or they're not.

Why waste extra time?

"I'm logged in," Amelia confirms, followed a minute later by, "Okay, you're all set with the boarding pass on the airline app and all that. Let me know if you need help figuring any of that out too."

"Thank you." She's babying me a little, but since it's my first time ever flying by myself, I'm happy to follow her lead. "How are finals?"

"Ugh, I need to get back to studying for my next exam, like, now."

I laugh. "Of course you do. Thanks for squeezing me in."

"Hey, don't worry, you'll be sick of me soon when we're stuck in the car crossing the country."

"I don't doubt it."

•••••

It's a dreary, rainy evening as I walk over to Roll Again. Peyton wanted to come playtest but had to cover a shift tonight for her cousin who flaked last minute. I'm carrying my game box wrapped in a garbage bag so I don't jumble all the work by carrying it sideways in my tote.

The cards turned out really nice, but the back image with witchy symbols printed a smidge blurry, which the preview online didn't indicate at all. The website customer service bot offered a partial refund but not a replacement.

Ah well. That's the vibe this project has, honestly.

If it wins, then my game will be produced professionally and look as beautiful as I know it can.

I went back and forth on the name but ultimately landed on Craft a Witch, which seems to fit this accusation-style blend of a party game pretty well. Besides Mafia/Werewolf, a game I could list as a reference title would probably be something like Clue, yet it really does feel too grand to try to compare my little creation to huge existing games that everyone knows and loves. I guess that's the only way for people to get a sense of what elements and gameplay to expect.

It does make me a little giddy, though, to imagine people playing this at Roll Again tonight and being like, *Wow, this is such a brilliant game.*

Even though it's probably trash.

The reality has to be somewhere in between, right?

The parking lot is more deserted than usual. Through the chiming door, I step inside and discover the small store is empty. Except for Declan, who is sitting on a stool behind the counter, wearing green today, hunched over a pile of dice and an even bigger notebook than his usual recordkeeping journal.

I clear my throat, but he doesn't look up. I walk all the way to the counter, and he still doesn't seem to notice me. "Hello?" I say.

Declan glances up but doesn't say anything.

"Isn't it a test run night?"

"Yep." He nods slowly, rearranging some of the dice in front of him into different piles, consulting an eight-by-eight-inch laminated chart of numbers, then adding a scoring token to a separate pile. I'm guessing this is his game creation. After taking his time with these calculations, he looks at me again. "You brought garbage?"

It takes a second for me to realize what he's referring to, and I quickly free Craft a Witch from its plastic-wrapped confines. ". . . It's raining."

"I could tell by your hair," Declan says. I'm unsure if it's supposed to be simply observational or mean.

I tuck a frizzy lock behind my ear, relieved my hearing aids have stayed relatively dry. "Whatever. Is anyone else coming to play?"

"I don't know. I don't think any of the other games are ready yet."

"Oh." I lower my box a few inches.

"I've got mine, though." Declan gestures to the mess of dice in front of him.

I frown. "Yeah, but mine needs at least four players. Five would be more ideal."

He taps his fingers on the counter, thinking for a second. "We could each play two turns so it's like there's four people."

"But it's sort of a mystery kind of game. If you know what another player's cards are, that takes away the guessing."

"I understand that; however, it is unfortunately our best option right now. We're just playing it as a test, not for actual fun, so it doesn't really matter if we don't get the full experience, does it?"

"I guess not," I grumble.

Declan slides his dice into a small nondescript box, folding the laminated chart inside, as well, and leads the way over to the wooden table in the corner, the one that stays up all the time, as opposed to all the extra folding tables that get brought out for things like Rivalry night.

"It's weird with no one else around." Sitting across from him, I'm unsure what else to say. We both have our boxes out on the table, but neither of us has a clear desire to be the one to open ourselves up to critique first.

"I've been alone in the store all afternoon. But now you're here." Declan doesn't look at me as he says that, staring down at his box of dice.

"Sorry to disturb your peace?"

I seriously don't know where I stand with this guy. I would guess we're acquaintances bordering on friends, if only because we've frequented the same spot for several years now, but if I were to refer to him outright as a friend, it would feel somewhat misleading.

Now we have to sit here cordially and each learn a brand-new game.

That's generally the biggest hurdle people have difficulty overcoming when first getting into board games. Learning a new rule book can feel frustrating and overwhelming, because you have to open your mind up to an unfamiliar experience.

But once you've figured out a game or two, you get the hang of the medium, and learning more board games becomes slightly easier when you're more comfortable with dice and cards and tokens and meeples and mechanisms.

I'm guessing most things in life are probably like this, and that once you get over initial hurdles, the journey is relatively smooth on the other side. Maybe that's how my hearing loss was. I got sick super young, so it's not something I remember well, but there must've been a bumpy adjustment period, learning to live life without an accustomed sense.

Yet if I have to experience losing a sense again, I doubt it will be an easier experience, so this probably isn't the best comparison. Just the topic I keep trying to shove to the back of my mind but that always manages to float its way to the surface.

Anyway, nothing and everything makes sense in life, but board game rules can be logical to figure out . . . if they were designed to be logical in the first place.

Which is to say that Declan's game, with its twenty-page rule book, makes no sense whatsoever.

"If you roll three matching pairs, you can swap to enter the third tier." He's in the midst of explaining, jamming a finger at a column on his laminated chart since consulting the list of figures is somehow integral to this gameplay. "Which, you know, has its benefits, but is a riskier gamble. Like, for example, it would be a safer bet to keep these in tier two, but over the course of the game, you're not going to be able to accumulate enough tokens if your opponent is playing a more offensive approach."

I reach forward and pick up a single die, my face contorted like I've tasted something sour. "What are you calling this game?"

"I'm submitting it with a working title."

"And that is?"

"Numbers."

My brows scrunch so far down that my eyes are almost closed. "I can't possibly have heard that right. You're calling this Numbers?"

"Yeah, it's growing on me, actually. Like, what else would I call it?" He smiles to himself as if it's some sort of silly personal joke.

"I honestly have no idea."

"Ready to play?" Declan is wide-eyed enthusiastic despite my blatant inability to hide my confusion. "Do the rules make sense?"

"Not at all," I say matter-of-factly.

"It's really not that hard," he insists, scooping up the rest of the thirty-something dice and nodding for me to open my hands to take all of them in addition to the one I'm already holding, which is pretty much the maximum number of dice I could possibly hold at once.

I sit, frozen, with all these dice held out in front of me. "Now what?"

He taps the table as if it's obvious. "Roll them."

"I assumed that much. But what's the deal with the chart?" I see him ready to launch into that full explanation from the top again, so I shake my head and roll all the dice onto the table. "No, just walk me through it as we play."

"Okay, so now that you've rolled, you pick an initial set," he says, sliding the chart toward me.

I don't mean to, but I laugh. "Declan, this is ridiculous."

There's a glint in his eyes as he smiles at me. When did Declan get taller? We used to sit eye to eye, but these days there's an uneven feeling across the playing table, as if height gives him an advantage. "It's really not that hard once you start to memorize the configurations," he says.

I chuckle again. "You want me to memorize this already? You know, I'm sure this game would have a very loyal niche following, but that's not likely to include me. The rules are a bit much, don't you think?"

"I am trying to find a way to cut a few pages from the instructions."

"A *few* would probably be helpful, yes. Or put a one-sheet up front that gives a general overview."

"It would be impossible to convey all the most important steps in a single page," he says, scratching his forehead.

I reach for the Craft a Witch box and retrieve my one-sheet instruction piece of cardstock. "It's possible."

"Hmm." He reads and rereads over the eight-point instructions. "There are the community tiles. Accusation cards. And then you take turns guessing and swapping, and . . . then what, exactly?"

"Oh." Even as I'm pulling the tiles out of the box to show him, I can feel the lack of tension in the player interactions within the rules for Craft a Witch. "I mean, it's like a party game, so the excitement is more what the players bring to it when they play." Declan nods along in uncertain agreement that makes me scrunch my brow. "But it feels too simple, doesn't it?"

Declan tilts his head, still staring at the rules card. "I didn't want to say it like that, but probably? There's still time to add an element or something that could pull through some higher stakes."

I sigh and cross my legs on the chair. "The problem is that I don't want to change anything at this point. Like, I'm turning it in because it's as good as it's going to get for now and I have to fly out of town tomorrow, so yeah, I don't know."

"I think it's probably good enough," Declan tries to reassure me.

"Yeah, and I didn't mean to be so hard on yours. You clearly put a lot of thought into developing that chart," I say, unable to resist another giggle as I point to the paper.

Fortunately, Declan smiles. "I'm going to go ahead and turn in mine too. I think we've both got strong contenders here." He reaches a hand across the table, and I cautiously extend mine to shake his. “Good luck.”

I smile. “May the best board game win.”

Although, since we both brought up fair critiques and yet are implementing absolutely *none* of the suggestions, I’ll be very surprised if either of our games makes it onto the podium.

Chapter Four

I'm stuck in the back of the airplane, waiting to disembark. It was a bumpy flight, and my stomach is rumbling. When it's my turn to get up, I rush down the empty aisle and turn onto the ramp, where there's a worker waiting with a wheelchair.

I do a double take at the sign they're holding up.

Because it has my name on it?

I'm in motion, and there's people behind me, so I don't want to stop or spin on my heels. I didn't request a wheelchair, nor do I need one. I continue walking and ignore the whole situation, wondering what the worker will think when the whole plane has cleared and no one has claimed the chair.

It's the first thing I discuss when I call my parents, their voices in my ears as I hold my phone in hand, walking away from the gate. "There was a wheelchair for me. That's so weird."

"There was a wheelchair?" Mom asks.

Maybe it's difficult to hear me over the airport chatter, but I don't want to shout about this, either.

"Yeah, with my name."

It doesn't take Mom long to figure it out. "You know what it might be? When I booked your ticket, I selected the Deaf or Hard of Hearing box."

"And they'd give me a wheelchair for that?"

"Who knows what services it automatically triggers in their system," she says. "Maybe it flags all accommodations similarly."

"Huh," Dad says. "Did you take the ride?"

"I'm regretting not considering it."

My phone buzzes with a text Mom sends to the family group chat. A picture from a road trip we took to Chicago when I was six and Amelia was seven. We're at a rest stop, standing in front of the car, wearing big cheesy grins and matching blue shirts covered in illustrated butterfly patterns, each holding a juice box in one hand and a cookie in the other.

It's also one of those photos where my first pair of hearing aids—hot pink with glittery ear molds—is very apparent, a sparkle of personality that my current pair doesn't display since they are tiny beige receivers tucked alongside my head with clear wiring that trails into my ears. Nearly invisible if I'm wearing my hair down, and only noticeable if you're looking closely when my hair is up.

My hearing loss is moderate, and I generally feel like I get by well enough on a day-to-day basis, though I'm curious to maybe find an American Sign Language class in college. I was intrigued to learn, but it took a back seat after Amelia's diagnosis—to the point where I'm not entirely sure how that would work for me anymore.

I rapidly weave through other travelers down the long corridor, and my mouth waters when I pass a cheesesteak shop, almost tempting me to grab some food for the road. "I'm still trying to find the exit."

"Call Amelia," Mom says. "She's almost there."

"Okay, I'll call her. Love you, bye."

After skipping past three bathrooms, I decide it's really best if I stop before getting in the car. At least it's easier to manage without a suitcase, though the first stall I try is missing a hook on the door to hang my backpack.

Then I'm still not sure where the exit is. I take a more leisurely pace as I turn the corner and call my sister.

"Where are you?" she asks. There's a loud horn obscuring her voice.

"I'm still inside. Trying to get to the exit where I can find you. I go toward baggage claim even if I didn't check a bag, right? Oh, ground transit—"

Because my brain is still thinking in board game creation, all of this feels like it could amount to some sort of journey-around-the-board-style game. In moments, I've pushed past the point of no return and find myself nearing the exit, where other travelers are standing around waiting for bags or outside waiting for ride pickups.

"Aah, I'm going to have to do a loop." Amelia continues grumbling incoherently as she struggles through airport traffic.

"Oh, you're like *here* here."

"Yeah, let's go."

"Okay, one second!"

I burst through the automatic doors. "I'm outside. Wearing bright pink."

"I'm already heading around now," Amelia says. "Less than a minute or so."

"Just slow down and I'll find you," I say, trying to figure out how to make this whole situation simpler for both of us. But that's easier said than done. There's a lot of cars slowing down. I finally spot Amelia, pulling over to the side, but she's pretty far away. "There you are!"

"They want me to move—hurry up!"

I take off, carefully speeding up as I jog down the sidewalk. "I'm running! I'm running!"

It's only when I'm about two feet away from the car that she says, "There you are!"

I open the door, my voice reverberating through the car's speakers. "No shit," I say before ending the call on my phone.

She smiles. "Hey."

Amelia looks like a college student. Specifically, one in the midst of exam week who's wearing Audubon College–branded sweats and could use a shower but is overcompensating with a heavy helping of apple-scented lotion. Her honey-blond hair is scrunched up into a knot atop her head, and she's wearing a star pimple patch beneath her chin. She's got the keys for the car in the center display, on a floral lanyard with her dorm room fob and a plastic case that holds her student ID for easy access.

"Hi." I fasten the seat belt and sit back into the seat. "The driver behind you has their signal on for you to get out of this spot."

The one accessory my sister is wearing that doesn't exactly scream typical college student is her bioptic telescopic driving glasses. While she doesn't use typical prescription lenses, the framed glasses—with two circular telescopes positioned above each eye—give her the ability to have a zoomed-in, closer look, which helps with reading street signs and observing traffic lights.

When she first got them, Dad made a joke that she looked like Inspector Gadget, and then we all went quiet because we weren't sure if she was going to be offended by that, but Amelia laughed and did not care. She was just relieved to have the opportunity to maintain her independence for as long as she can.

Even though I told her we were clear to merge over, Amelia still checks each mirror several times, testing everyone's, but most especially my stomach's, patience.

"Do you want me to drive to campus?" I offer.

She moves over into the next lane. "No, I know these roads."

My stomach roars. "Whoa, hungry much?"

"You could hear that?"

"Possibly the loudest sound I've ever heard. We can get dinner on campus."

I let her focus on the road until we're out of the airport mess and into smooth sailing on the highway. "Hey." I start the hellos again, because I haven't seen my sister in person since December.

It's her turn to say hi.

"That's all you've got?" I tease. "You made me fly all this way and go on a multiday drive back home just to spend some time with you, and all you've got is *hi*?"

"How was your flight?" Then she giggles at the second mundane conversation starter. "Sorry, my brain has been locked in on anthropology for the last seventy-two hours. That exam had no business being that difficult, but it was even worse than I expected."

"You've still got another test tomorrow?"

"Actually, two, but these last ones aren't tests. One is a group presentation for a communications class, and the other we have to show up to turn in the final paper because the professor refuses to accept online submissions. It'll be an easier day tomorrow. We can hang. You can help me pack. We're still on track to hit the road Wednesday and get home late Thursday night."

She's forgetting the next step of her itinerary.

"And then you flee the country," I say, thinking of next week.

"Jealous? You should come visit."

Her program offers a study abroad course, which sounds like one giant vacation to me, in an I'm-definitely-jealous sort of way. She'll be at a college in Spain but will be getting to travel to several other European countries as well, which makes sense because everything's so close together over there. The point is to learn to communicate or something? I don't really understand what a communications major is, to be honest.

•••••

We finally approach her school, and from the road around the perimeter of Audubon College, I get a peek at the campus. The hilly green quad and the old brick buildings. Students who are trudging to an exam in stark contrast to their peers who are walking out to summer freedom. Amelia continues to drive us around the outskirts to a super-faraway parking structure in the back, where she winds through the garage until we finally find empty spaces on the top level.

"They started letting freshmen have cars like a year or two ago," she explains. "This was the only spot they had to build more parking, which they are definitely overcharging us for, like everything else. I get by well enough with transit or catching rides with friends, so you can keep the car next year."

"That's so kind of you." My voice is laced with sarcasm. "That's always been the plan, but I'm glad you think it was your decision."

She scrunches up her nose gleefully. "Just saying it works out for both of us."

"That's good. Don't go changing your mind. Do I get to keep the lanyard too?"

"No. A friend gave me that. You can buy your own."

She parks the car, and someone quickly takes the empty space beside us. The girl glances over and smiles at Amelia, but Amelia gives a blank look in response. Perhaps not recognizing the person, which doesn't mean it's not someone she knows.

"Amelia!" the girl shouts out, waving, probably thinking my sister is spacey or something.

Amelia recognizes her voice and cracks open the door. "Camila! Hey!" She scrambles to take off her driving lenses and put them away.

But Camila notices. "Nice glasses," she says, in a way that fortunately seems more curious than mean.

Amelia shrugs it off, deflecting with an "oh, ha, yeah, no" as she quickly puts them away in their case without further explanation, swaps on a pair of regular sunglasses, and changes the subject with "This is my little sister."

We climb out of the car. "*Younger* sister. I stopped being your *little* sister years ago." I smile at her friend. "Hey, I'm Iris."

"Yeah, Iris." Camila nods. She's in an oversized pair of dark overalls and a light blue baseball hat, with a thick braid hanging over one shoulder while her nearly empty backpack is slung over the other. She's clutching her similar mess of car-and-campus-related keys on a lanyard matching Lee's. "Amelia talks about you all the time. Y'all look so similar."

"We get that a lot," I say.

"I gotta run to a final," Camila says, but she pauses to ask, "Catch you later? You're not heading out soon, right?"

"Yeah, Wednesday," Amelia answers. "We'll see you before then. But also . . . next week!"

Both girls give enthusiastic squeals of excitement before Camila rushes off to her exam.

I step back to the passenger side to grab my stuff, slightly embarrassed to be walking around campus with a bag this full to the brim. "Is that one of your close friends? You've definitely mentioned her before."

"Yeah, Camila. She's great."

Studying Amelia's face, I ask, "But she hadn't seen your bioptics?"

"Nah, she usually offers to drive when we go off campus."

"Why don't you ever drive?"

"Because I'd rather be a passenger princess."

I shake my head and fall into step with my sister as she leads us out of the parking lot and onto a campus path. The abundance of greenery on this walkable path away from cars is a refreshing change of pace. "I'm not doing the entire twenty hours back home."

"Of course not."

"But she doesn't know what your glasses are for?" I ask, not able to shake that exchange from my mind.

"I don't actually wear *glasses*," she says, stuck on the distinction, as if I need reminding. But, like, wouldn't her friend know why Amelia has these special lenses for driving?

"Have you not told your new friends about your vision?"

Amelia shrugs, indifferent. "No."

I don't understand how something like this doesn't come up in conversation eventually. "Why not?"

She quickens her pace, and I have to fight to keep up while carrying this heavy bag and walking side by side enough so that I can read her lips as we talk. She answers with a question of her own: "Why do they need to know?"

"Huh?"

"Like, do you tell every person you ever meet about your hearing aids?"

That feels different, if only because everyone in my life has known me since I was a little kid, when the hearing aids I wore were a lot more visibly apparent. My recent pair isn't obvious, so I guess I will probably have to explain when I go to college and meet new people.

"I've never really thought about it," I admit.

Amelia is blind similar to the way I'm deaf—neither one of us is living in complete darkness or silence. Deafness and blindness are spectrums, which can confuse people when they meet those of us who don't embody classic stereotypes.

For some reason, all the gray area in between *this* and *that* is too complicated for many to understand, even though that's the reality for much of life. There's something simplistic and soothing about categorizing things, which therefore leads to agitation or even fear when other peoples' lives don't fit squarely into easily conceptualized boxes.

Specifically, Amelia has Stargardt's, which is a rare genetic disease otherwise referred to as juvenile macular degeneration. It's a progressive loss of central vision, so over time she'll lose more and more of her sight. Typically, peripheral vision remains unaffected, which leaves some usable vision, but the tricky part is that things you see in your periphery aren't in full focus.

I've tried to ask Amelia to describe what it looks like through her eyes, but she usually explains it simply as *My brain fills in the gaps.*

With her current level of vision, if there are a few things on a table in front of her, she'll generally know where they are but not be able to discern exactly *what* they are until a closer inspection. Familiar things in expected places are easier to identify, whereas for something unexpected, she usually has to hold it up pretty close to her face to get the full picture. Reading text is often the most difficult aspect, and she has several apps for magnifying or reading aloud.

It was a learning curve for me to figure out when I could be helpful versus when I was overstepping. Easy assistance like reading scene cards or foreign language subtitles on a TV show out loud for her became second nature for me when she still lived at home, but trying to rush her or do something for her when she could do it herself with extra time to look closely was a big no.

The suggested course of action is to get regular eye exams, wear sunglasses, avoid too much vitamin A, and not smoke.

As of now, there's no treatment or cure.

"Remember the dining hall?" Amelia points to our left, though I don't remember this exact building. "This is the smaller one on North Campus."

"I was going to say, I don't remember this one from the tour."

When we dropped her off in August, I went on an official campus tour with our parents even though I already knew the schools I was applying to and had been on so many different campus tours that they all blurred together. Still, it was nice to see where my sister was going to be living.

"Well, now I'll give you the *real* tour," she says. "The dining hall sucks. But the nook by the library, which is still on the meal plan, is excellent. I've got swipes left—want a bagel?"

"Yes, please."

The cafeteria is a kind-of-grimy, low-lit, tucked-away spot with only three small tables and a deli counter, but it has the sort of vibe where I can already tell the food is going to be great.

"What do you want?" she asks.

"I don't know. Whatever you get."

She goes up to the counter while I grab us a spot at the only open table by the window.

It's still weird to me that she's hiding her vision loss from the people she's met at college. Wouldn't it be easier if they knew? It feels like Amelia is running away from something, desperate to be someone new.

Anyway, I don't think I would hide a diagnosis like that. Not from friends. But I'm not in that position, exactly.

At least not yet.

It all comes down to that freaking 25 percent chance.

The likelihood that I'll also inherit Stargardt disease. Amelia's condition is genetic, and it's somewhat common for it to affect siblings.

Parents are usually unaffected carriers, but each of their children has a one-in-four chance to inherit. There's new genetic testing that could be done to try to determine if I'll develop it, but the doctors don't recommend it as long as I'm still asymptomatic. A test wouldn't change anything about how we'd react to an early diagnosis right now because of the whole *no cure* thing, so it's usually reserved for the point in time when it could confirm a diagnosis rather than foresee one.

How would I react to knowing this might be inevitable?

It can be hard to keep the anxiety at bay. Knowing there's literally nothing I can do to change a potential predetermined outcome.

Would I handle it as well as Amelia seems to be? How would I balance losing sight with my existing hearing loss?

Although, there's a 75 percent chance I *don't* get it. Shouldn't I find that relaxing to hold on to rather than freaking out about the odds that I do?

Amelia grabs food at the counter and turns around, not knowing exactly where I've sat or at which table. For a second, she looks directly at me, not fully *seeing* me, as she scans the other bodies in the room.

It's strange to have this rare diagnosis on my radar, with the fear of the unknown, while at the same time already watching my sister's experience.

"Lee," I call out. She hurries over, following my voice without missing a step, taking the opposite chair and sliding my bagel across the table.

She scrambles to unwrap the sandwich parchment, smiling wide. "Get ready for the best bagel of your life."

Chapter Five

Tuesday afternoon I stroll around the quad in front of the building that Amelia ran in to drop off her last final assignment, but it's been twenty minutes and there's no sign of her yet. It's entirely possible the professor made them stay for something or she's chatting with a friend; either way, I don't know whether I'm stuck here for a few more minutes, or even hours if the professor is keeping them for the entire scheduled exam period duration.

It's a nice spring day. Sixty degrees that is almost too warm but will soon be a distant dream when the sweltering summer heat emerges in full force. The campus is quieter than I last saw it during the hustle and bustle of freshman move-in because everyone's studying or taking tests or finishing up last-minute papers or lucky enough to already be on summer vacation but still hanging around here with friends. I sit on a bench right outside the relatively newer 1980s-style building, waiting for my sister and wondering if I look like a college student already.

Because in three months, I will be.

With my own bed in my own dorm room, though. Not sharing a twin mattress with Amelia like last night. My sister still kicks in her sleep. There are some things that time can never change. Her roommate is leaving today, so I'll get the spare bed tonight, at least.

A set of lost parents wanders by. I don't hear them at first, but they approach me. "Excuse me, can you point us to the dining hall? Our son is in an exam, and we're looking for something to eat."

I stand—not sure why, except it feels more efficient to do so while pointing. "The dining hall is that way." I gesture very vaguely, hoping they don't ask for more specifics, because I don't have them. Instead, I offer, "But the food at the nook by the library is really good."

"Oh, we just saw the library. Let's try that," the wife says, patting her husband's arm. "Thank you," she says to me as they walk away.

I sit back down and scroll through my phone before deciding it's much more interesting to people watch. A few dudes have commandeered a large portion of the quad to play Frisbee. Some sorority girls in matching T-shirts hurry past, all talking over each other, excitedly making plans. A professor with no fewer than five tote bags slung over their shoulders takes a final bite of an apple before tossing it in the trash. And walking this way is a guy with floppy dark hair who kind of looks like Declan.

I blink and shake my head, turning to look the other direction. Why am I seeing his face? The way he's been keeping track of all my match losses must really be doing a number on me.

Technically, it's our wins side by side, but that feels like giving him too much credit.

"Iris?" The guy who looks like Declan is standing right in front of me.

It *is* Declan.

The confirmed recognition lights up in his crinkling eyes. "Couldn't go a Tuesday without seeing me?"

He's not in one of his usual hoodies, which must've thrown me off. We're both cosplaying college students and stepping out of our usual attire. I borrowed sweats from Amelia's closet, while Declan is wearing a loose brown T-shirt, and for some reason, it draws my attention right to his arms.

"Um, Declan?" My eyes narrow as I jump to my feet. Should I swipe the air to make sure he's not some sort of twisted mirage?

Before I can fully comprehend what's happening, he's holding his arms out wide, and I instinctively greet him with a hug. My thoughts immediately cascade with further confusion. We're hugging. We hug now? In all the years we've known each other, I've never hugged this boy before.

"What are you doing here?" I ask.

He takes a seat on the bench, so I lower back to where I was sitting. "I was about to ask you that," he says.

My cheeks flush, and I feel caught out somehow, even though I have a perfectly legitimate reason for being here. "I'm picking up my sister."

"I'm here to get my brother."

I'm growing more baffled by this outcome. "I didn't even know you had a brother. A freshman?"

"Sophomore," he says. "I knew you had a sister because she used to show up to Roll Again when you first started playing. She's just a year older than us, right?"

We lock eyes. My chin juts forward, shoulders hunched. I don't know if I should laugh or cry or call my mom. "Okay, seriously, I feel like I'm being pranked."

He slides across the bench, staring straight ahead at the quad as he leans his head toward my shoulder while asking "How so?"

If I turn, I'll be right on top of him. I look ahead as well. "What are the odds that you and I are going to the same college *and* our siblings go to the same school too? This doesn't feel probable in the slightest."

He clicks his tongue, sitting upright, seeming to be seriously considering this calculation. "Probably not *that* statistically significant, although there's a handful of schools that Midwest kids usually end up at. Though this small college isn't really one of them." He scratches the edge of his lips with his thumb. "Pretty unlikely, I have to admit. A rare occurrence."

I make a sour face for the briefest moment. I think I catch myself quickly enough, trying to return to a neutral expression, but Declan notices, and I hope he doesn't assume it has anything to do with him.

"What?" he asks.

"I just—I don't like rare odds."

"Why not?" He leans forward, almost giddy. "I think it's cool. Of all the college campuses across the country, of all the days of the week and the hours in a day, you and I ended up sitting here together right now." Seriously, he's such a nerd.

"Maybe to *you* it seems like a cool thing. But to me it's proof that just because something is unlikely doesn't mean that it won't happen."

"Did I tell you I'm majoring in statistics?" Another cheeky grin. It's weird seeing a whole new side of Declan. He's smiling so much. Too much.

It's contagious, so I smile too. "Of course you are. I'm very familiar with your love of numbers." I gesture from us to the campus and back to me and him. "Then tell me—what exactly are the odds that you ended up in front of me right now?"

"No idea," he says. "I'll have to take a class and let you know." I lean forward to shove him for being preposterous, and he laughs, eager to latch on to my hands and playfully push back. "What about you? What are you going to study?"

I sit back and readjust my hair as if just now remembering where I am and who exactly I'm sitting next to. "History."

"That makes complete sense, as well."

"I suppose it does."

"You want to learn how things went in the past and then try to figure out how they'll go in the future?"

I shake my head. Flushed, I admit, "It does seem a comforting way to look at things, but that's not exactly how it works. History *rhymes* rather than repeats."

"Someone got a head start on their summer reading," he teases, though he seems impressed.

We sit in silence for a moment until Declan finds another question. "Well, is it a nice rhyme that you and I are together again on a Tuesday?"

"I've never seen you outside Roll Again."

"I practically live there. I'm going to miss it."

I remind him, "There's still game nights when you're home for break."

He gets a faraway look in his eyes, like that might not be possible, before suggesting something else. "I'm sure we'll find somewhere cool in Indy, though."

We'll find someplace cool. I didn't realize how much of a relief it would be to have someone I know going to the same school as me.

Even if that someone is Declan.

I'm wrapped up in this conversation and don't notice at first that Amelia has stepped out of the building and is looking around for me. She's stopped to pull out her phone.

"Lee! Over here." I don't stand from the bench yet.

"Your sister?" Declan asks, not entirely a question, because she is so obviously related to me.

"Yeah, it's Amelia," I say.

"That took forever." She rushes over. "I'm sorry you had to wait. The professor made us watch this pointless video." Amelia nods toward Declan, her protective-older-sister persona emerging as she wonders who this dude is hanging out next to me. "But you found someone to talk to?"

It's hard for her to see faces, so even if she would've recognized him—which is doubtful, because it's been ages and at least one major growth spurt since she went to a game night—she definitely wouldn't be able to place him out of context. I say, "Do you remember Declan Weber? He also hangs out at Roll Again Games?"

"Wow, Declan!" she says. "Your voice sounds so different. The last time I saw you, you weren't so grown-up."

"Okay, Mom," I say.

She shrugs. "College makes it feel like much more time has passed."

Declan laughs. "I'm sure. It's nice to see you again. Iris and I were talking about how random it is to run into each other here."

"He's here to get his brother," I explain.

"Do you know Grady Weber?" Declan asks.

Amelia shakes her head. "Can't say that rings a bell."

"He's a year older," Declan says, "so you might not have crossed paths."

"You're here to fly back with him?" Amelia asks.

"Actually, we're driving," Declan says. "Probably heading out later today or tomorrow."

My jaw goes slack. "How do you not know when you're leaving? Don't you have a hotel booked?"

He shrugs. "Nah, on road trips we just stop wherever and find a place."

"How do you live that way?" I shake my head. "Assuming all the pieces will just fall into place? I could never do that—are you kidding me? What if there's not a hotel nearby? Or they don't have a room available? Or—"

But Declan just grins, amused to watch me ramble again. "It always seems to work out."

I roll my eyes. "Of course it does. For *you*."

Amelia speaks over my muttering. "We're driving back to Omaha too! We should caravan!"

"Wait, I—"

Declan is quick to agree. "That could be fun. I'll ask my brother. When are you guys heading out?"

"Tomorrow morning," Amelia says.

I continue my halfhearted protest. "I think it's actually safer to not, like, follow behind another car."

Wait, why am I against this? If everyone else is on board, then I can go along with it. Yet it dawns on me that this brief encounter with Declan is potentially turning into an entire journey, and I'm not sure I'm equipped to handle that.

"Don't worry. I drive safe," he says. "Grady would call it too slow . . . but I'll make sure he keeps his foot off the gas when it's his turn behind the wheel."

Amelia takes out her phone and types a text. From the vibration in my pocket, I suspect it was sent to me, telling me to chill.

I take the hint. "Yeah, that's fine."

Both Declan and I get up from the bench at the same time. I take a few steps backward to physically align myself with Amelia rather than him.

"Perfect," Amelia says in the kind of older sibling tone that finalizes the matter at hand. "Text Iris and we'll coordinate a time."

"Later," I say, trying to scrutinize his face for any trace of similar apprehension.

"Yeah, see ya soon." He holds his hand up as a goodbye.

As Amelia and I walk away, I find myself annoyed. This was supposed to be a trip with just my sister and me on the open road, after all.

"He's calling for you," Amelia says, nudging my arm.

"What?" I stop and turn around, nearly crashing into Declan as he jogs after us. Amelia stands a few feet ahead, waiting, and I can sense a smirk on her face. One that I just *know* will amount to a comment later.

Why does everything about this feel so embarrassing?

"Um." Declan's shoulders shrug up to his ears. "I've known you since we were twelve, but I don't actually have your number . . . which seems easier than trying to message you on the store's group chat board."

"Oh, right." Without thinking too much, I hand over my cell.

His cheeks burn bright red as he takes my phone, inputs his number, and sends a message to himself. While handing it back, he says, "There was a text from your sister waiting for you to read or something . . ."

Declan walks off in the opposite direction before I have a chance to discover what my sister sent me earlier.

Amelia: Relax, the drive will be fun. What, do you have a crush on him or something?

I storm over to Amelia. "Oh my god, Lee. That *text?*" She doesn't immediately recollect, or pretends not to, so I remind her. "The text you sent me that *he just saw*." My voice goes up an octave, and I glance behind to make sure he's out of earshot. He's strolling away with his hands in his pockets, not seeming to have a destination in mind. I spin around, worried he'll feel me staring. I tap Amelia's elbow to signal that we should start moving again, and quickly. "I most definitely *do not* have a crush on Declan Weber."

"I don't know." She raises her hands, all innocent, as we walk away. "You were acting strange."

"Because you just invited these guys to drive all the way home with us? That wasn't the plan."

She shrugs. "It seems like it could be fun. We have our own car; we can go our separate ways at any point."

"Maybe it could've been fun if he hadn't just seen that ridiculous message you sent? Now he's going to think I have a crush on him. And like I said, I don't!"

"You're protesting a little too much."

"Oh my gosh," I say, my cheeks bright red. "Because when you deny an accusation, it just makes people think you're lying for some reason, even when you're absolutely telling the truth.

That's like a whole big component of the board game I just designed!"

"I really had no idea he would see that text. That's on you for handing over your phone without checking it first."

I groan, exasperated. "Great. All this right before we're apparently driving the whole way back though Pennsylvania"—I start spouting off states for dramatic emphasis—"Ohio, Indiana, Illinois, Iowa, *and* Nebraska with him and his brother."

"Wow, we won't even need a map."

I continue whining, fully aware that I sound like a petulant child. "Amelia!"

"Like I said, they'll be in a different car. It's totally fine."

"Then what's the point of even driving together?"

"Because we'll have more people to talk to when we're at rest stops after being stuck in a car just the two of us for hours and hours and h—"

"Okay, fine!" I cut her off, since the teasing gleam in her eyes suggests she'll continue indefinitely if I don't. "If you insist."

"You are being weird." Her voice slips into a sincerity we don't often broach. "Because you *do* like him . . ."

"No, I don't—I don't know, he's like . . . my rival?" I cringe the second I say it. But it's true. We regularly play against each other in a board game, a long-standing matchup in which he's compelled to tally our wins and losses. That seems like a basic definition of *rivals* to me.

Amelia makes an *aww* face that makes me want to puke. "Aww, like, rivals who play Rivalry. That's the most adorable shit I've ever heard."

"This is mortifying."

I'm sure I could easily clear up this misunderstanding. He apparently has an older brother. He has to understand sibling teasing.

I think back to the text. I suppose what's really bothering me right now is that our playing field is totally uneven. It's like another tally in his notebook of match victories. He's probably feeling smug and assuming I've been harboring some sort of secret unrequited crush. I can't stand Declan thinking he's somehow got the upper hand.

Chapter Six

While Amelia sorts though clothes in her closet, I'm tasked with taking down her decorations. There's a little string of photographs spanning the wall above her bed, with the images she brought from home and put up on move-in day. There's one of her at an amusement park with her high school friends. At her graduation with our grandparents. Smiling with Mom and Dad on her birthday. The two of us at the lake.

Then, on the wooden wardrobe doors on the wall by this dorm room's central mirror vanity, she's collected a series of more updated images from her time in college so far, Camila being the friend that features most prominently in both group and solo shots. I carefully remove the tape from the back of each image and stack the four-by-sixes into a neat little pile.

"I forgot I had this." Amelia holds up a gold dress. "Why did I ever think I would need this on campus?"

"You didn't have any formal events?" I ask, grabbing the spare set of sheets and fitting them onto her roommate's vacant bed.

"I did, but none that I wanted to wear my old homecoming dress to." She laughs and tosses it into her suitcase.

I lie down on my freshly made bed and pull out my phone under the guise of not wanting to get in her way until she needs my help packing, but also to text my friends, since there's been messages piling up in the group chat for a while now.

Elizabeth: I got my roommate assignment. Aah, is this going to be terrible?

Peyton: What do you know about her??

Elizabeth: Just that she's also majoring in music and is from New Jersey? Peyton, are people from NJ nice??

Peyton: I'm only going to school there–I can't vouch for all the people

Elizabeth: Like, why does she want to be a Cornhusker?

Peyton: Sounds like a perfect first question to email her

Elizabeth: I have to be the one to email first??

Peyton: Do you have her info? Can we stalk her??

This continues for no fewer than four hundred messages, where my friends try to find out as much as they can about Elizabeth's new roommate, Olivia Sullivan, a girl whose name is common enough to return several thousand search results for about a million different people.

I filled out my own roommate-match questionnaire a few weeks ago, and now I'm regretting how indecisive I was when answering it. Do I like to stay up late? Sometimes. Do I listen to music when I study? Sometimes. Do I like to have friends over? Sometimes.

I have no idea who they're going to stick me with.

I've already spent most of my life living with a roommate, and I'm looking right at her. Amelia has given up on carefully folding things into organized piles on her bed and is grabbing armfuls of clothing to dump on the bedspread and sort out later, triggering the memory of the one relief that came from Amelia leaving for college, which was not having to trip over my sister's dirty laundry anymore. She leaves piles for days, and it was tough to have to resort to a sniff test to determine if a shirt of hers I wanted to borrow was from a clean or dirty stack.

I give up trying to read through the backlog of my friends' text messages, because there are more arriving every second.

Iris: I'm here!!! Did you find THE Olivia??

Elizabeth: No. I'm going to have to email her

Peyton: Just be like, "Hey I'm your roommate," and then make her tell you about herself first. You don't want to come on too strong

Elizabeth: I know right–like, are we going to be friends or is she going to hate me???

Peyton: You are the definition of nice. There's no way anyone would hate you

Iris: You're lucky you're rooming with your friend from camp

Peyton: Yeah, I already know Alaiya is cool:)

For as long as I've known her, Peyton has spent a week every summer at a camp for epileptic kids. Pairing up with a college roommate you're already friends with, and who's in the same boat and won't be uninformed and freaked out by the possibility of a seizure, makes a lot of sense.

I'm curious if I'll have a disabled roommate, too, because I requested accommodations for the deaf fire alarm that has flashing strobe lights. Apparently, campuses tend to only outfit a certain number of rooms as accessible dorms, so that seems to increase the odds exponentially that the disabled kids would room together.

Elizabeth: Iris, how's college??

Iris: Weird, actually. Um, guess who I ran into?

Peyton: Ummmm, your sister

Elizabeth: Who?!

Iris: Declan

Peyton: Ha! He can start tallying all the places you've seen each other now

Elizabeth: Wait, this is scorekeeping guy??

I stifle a giggle. Peyton and I have been ragging on him a little bit, but in a somewhat endearing way mostly, which has made

Elizabeth really curious what the situation here is. I'm equally inquisitive, to say the least.

Iris: He's going to major in statistics

Peyton: Sure

Elizabeth: What's he doing there??

Iris: Oh yeah, he's here for his brother and we're now apparently driving all the way back home with them

Peyton: No offense, but that's way more interesting than talking about his statistics major.
You should've started with that.

Elizabeth: Send me a picture of this guy.
I forget what he looks like!

Peyton starts spamming the chat with screenshots of a few pictures that have been uploaded to the store's message board over the years. Lots of blurry photos of people hunched over tables playing board games. Nothing flattering of Declan . . . or me, for that matter.

Iris: At least find something from his social media

Peyton: Do you follow him??

Iris: Yeah, but he never really posts

I know. I've recently checked.

Amelia pulls out an ugly neon green sweatshirt from one of her drawers. It has a faded Kermit the Frog on the front and is so comfortable, and I love it, and it's been missing from my life for too long.

"Hey! You stole that," I say. "I've been wondering where it went."

"Well, since it's mine, it got packed and brought to college." She holds her arm up high, out of reach, and dangles it in the air.

"You're definitely misremembering something."

She shakes her head and tosses the sweatshirt to me. "I didn't end up wearing it, so it can be yours."

I hug the fabric tight to my chest. "Like it always was . . ."

Iris: Hey, I gotta help pack now

Peyton: Keep us updated

Elizabeth: And send a better photo of him!!

Iris: No, I'm not going to take a random picture of this boy?

I slide my phone into my pocket and jump up to help Amelia, who is standing on her toes trying to inch another big suitcase out from overhead in the closet with just her fingertips. I'm ever so slightly taller than her these days, but it doesn't make much of a difference. Nevertheless, we hoist it down to the ground, and she unzips it, frowning at the couple of sweaters that are already inside.

"Maybe I should've had you fly with an empty suitcase so I had more room to pack things."

"Yeah, cause TSA would love that," I say. "It was pretty incredible going through the airport without any luggage other than my backpack." I walk over to the counter where her roommate left behind extra cleaning supplies and grab a trash bag from the box. "Good thing you can just throw everything in some of these and fill up the car trunk."

"I guess so."

Amelia tosses a few T-shirts in my direction. I put them into the bag and throw the entire thing back at her, but she's already turned back to the closet, so it bounces off her butt and falls to the ground. Very helpful of me.

•••••

It takes us a few more hours before Amelia's entire college existence is consolidated into movable bags and boxes, aside from the pajamas and toiletries and things we'll need for tonight and the drive home. We crash together on the floor, sitting along the wall, feasting on the remnants of food from her snack box and rented mini fridge.

"At least your exam week was pretty short," I say, grabbing a handful of pretzel sticks.

"Well, I was supposed to have a test on Thursday and another on Friday, but those professors both wanted to start summer early, so they gave us the tests during the final class period instead of the scheduled exam period."

"I'd definitely prefer that."

"It was a unanimous vote." Amelia sniffs the yogurt before searching around for a plastic utensil.

"Talk about class solidarity." I glance around the room. "I'm glad we had some time without your roommate."

With the spoon in her mouth, Amelia widens her eyes and nods. "Me too."

"She seemed nice enough yesterday, but you made her sound like the worst."

"Yeah, as a person, she was mostly fine . . . but as a roommate, you don't even know the half of it." I'm ready for more of the horror stories, even if they're just a rehashing of the ones she told me throughout the year, particularly the moldy shower caddy one, because Amelia's retelling would be so much more expressive now that we're sitting here together. "Ah well, I'll probably never run into her again."

It's strange to think about living with someone for an entire school year and then just never seeing them again. "Really?"

"Yeah, we're different majors. Maybe we'll nod hello as we cross on the quad, but I doubt I'll see her intentionally. Just glad we made it through this year in one piece."

"Elizabeth got her roommate assignment today. But I won't find out about mine until later this summer."

"You could get lucky and end up with your own room."

I tilt my head, not following what she's saying. "Why would I get my own room?"

"If they put you in one of those accommodations rooms but there's an uneven number of students eligible for them."

Glancing up to the two beds in this dorm, I acknowledge that it would be nice to have extra space to myself, but it nags at me too. "That seems lonely. I mean, it seems better than a bad roommate, *for sure*, but at the same time, if everyone else has a roommate, it would be strange to be the only one without one."

"That probably won't happen." Amelia nods multiple times, like a school counselor offering reassurance to a problem you hadn't even anticipated would be a problem until she brought it up. "Just a possibility."

"True. Did you get to pick your roommate for next year?"

"Yeah, Camila and I requested each other."

I'm about to ask if we should see if Camila is around to hang out tonight when Amelia says, "Have you texted your boyfriend about tomorrow yet?"

I give a stern look. "Let's get one thing straight. Not a *single* joke like that on the drive."

"Just saying, you knew exactly who I was talking about . . ."

"You know it's a joke, and I know it's a joke, but how is Declan supposed to know it's a joke?"

"You could tell him. Just be forthright and break his heart."

I roll my eyes. "What? That makes no sense, because I guarantee he doesn't like me like that either."

"That you know of," Amelia says with a smirk.

"Let me check if he messaged," I mutter, pulling my phone from my pocket, partially hoping he did send a text, but one explaining that he and his brother were going to drive on their own and that we didn't actually commit to caravaning across the country earlier today.

Alas, Declan did send me a couple texts fifteen minutes ago.

Declan: What time should we meet tomorrow morning?

Declan: Also, we're in Delancey 317 with too much pizza if you guys want to swing by

"What's your dorm called?" I ask Amelia.

"Franklin."

"They're in Delancey. With extra pizza."

She immediately gives up on the last of her yogurt. "I knew you should've texted sooner. You're about to discover the *best* part of college."

"And what's that?"

"Free food, of course."

"Why even bother with the meal plan?" I ask.

"Because they make it mandatory."

We spring into action. Amelia gathers up the trash while I clip closed the pretzel and chip bags for us to bring on the road tomorrow. It's exhilarating to be walking distance from hanging out with people on campus rather than having to commute somewhere to see friends like I do back home.

She slips on her Audubon College sweatshirt while I mess with my hair in the mirror. Does up or down scream more casual? And why do I even care? It's not like I've ever put extra effort into how I look when I show up for game nights.

Yet we're a long way from Roll Again.

"You know where this room is?" I ask.

"Camila lives in that building. I texted her that we're heading over that way. It's not too far from here."

Iris: All right, we'll be there soon!

Can figure out tomorrow then

Declan: Nice

"Here." Amelia throws me the Kermit sweatshirt. "You'll be cold."

"I thought you deemed this un-collegiate."

"You're not a college student yet," she says. I hesitate, not sure I actually want to wear this on campus, but she insists. "Since you missed it so much. Put it on already. Come on."

I slide it over my head, careful not to mess up my ponytail. I reach over and grab Amelia's lanyard of keys, which she left on the table in front of the mirror, where I see myself. I have to admit this might be the perfect *I don't care what anyone thinks of me now that I'm in college* look.

"I'm pulling it off," I tell Amelia, in case she needs assistance with the full visual of my attire.

"I'm *sure* you are," she responds with unclear sincerity. Too late to change now. Amelia is already out in the hallway, and I rush after her, letting the door lock behind us.

"So, we're just going to go hang out with Declan and his brother?" I ask.

"Well, you are," she says. I'm not sure what she means, so I wait for her to explain further. "One of Camila's friends is having a going-away party on a different floor, so it actually works out well for me. I'll swing by that with her really quick."

I walk a few steps down the dorm hallway in silence. "A going-away party? Aren't you all leaving to go home for the summer?"

"The friend is transferring to a different school, so I should probably stop by there tonight."

When I finally realize exactly what's happening, I try to find a way to ask this question that doesn't sound like I'm about to go running off tattling to our parents. "You're just dropping me off at some guy's dorm?"

Amelia gives me a pointed look. "It's your friend? Would you rather hang around with a bunch of strangers you don't know?"

"No, but—"

"Come on, it's going to be fun! You can get a taste of the college experience."

This hallway stretches on forever. We pass a few other students on their way out somewhere tonight, as well. "Which is what?"

"Sitting around in some dorm eating pizza."

"It really is all about food, isn't it?"

"And I won't be out too late since we have to leave pretty early tomorrow."

"Okay, sure." There's ample attitude in my response.

Amelia stops walking to look right at me, head tilted ever so slightly so I'm in her periphery, giving me a chance to tell her how I really feel. "That's fine, right?" she asks. "Really, since they're in the same building, it just seems like such an easy way for us to do both, but if you don't want to hang out with

Declan or don't want me to go to the party, we can reconfigure, no problem."

I consider this. Amelia and I have already spent most of today together, and we'll have lots of time on the drive home, and we already text and call each other most days. Even if those interactions feel brief, at least we're generally always in contact.

But part of me wants to know for sure that, even now that our lives are diverging, my sister would choose to hang out with me. Not just because I was always a default available option, the younger sibling she *had* to spend time with.

That being said, I am curious for a taste of what college will be like. Knowing Amelia will be easily reachable on a different floor feels like a perfect safety net.

"No, you're right, it's fine. Works out well that it's in the same building." I parrot her words, not really having any other strong sentiments to share with her on the matter.

Chapter Seven

It takes less than three minutes to walk over to Delancey Hall, where Camila is waiting for us in the lobby on onc of the faded yellow chairs lined up against the entryway window. There's a student working the front desk, scanning IDs and collecting guest names on a sign-in sheet. I have to flip to a fresh page, since all the rows on the first one are already full with names of visitors during these final days of the semester.

Camila has applied fresh makeup for the night, her hair teased back. Amelia leans over and whispers in her ear, something that makes Camila's face contort with amused disbelief. Both girls laugh.

"What was that?" I ask.

"Nothing," my sister says. I can tell it wasn't about me, so I don't press. She turns to me. "What was Declan's brother's name again? Maybe Camila knows him."

"Grady," I say.

"Oh, yeah, on the sophomore floors?" Camila says. "He's, uh, nice enough, I guess."

That's such a vague response that could indicate a million different things, most of which are not great. I ask, "What does that mean?"

"Poli sci major," Camila continues, as if that explains everything. By the knowing look on Amelia's face, maybe it does.

Camila leads us down a hallway, past a long row of mailboxes and a package-collection counter that has a line of students waiting for the cardboard boxes crowding the small storage room. I'm falling behind, needing to crane my neck to follow their conversation as we walk down the hall at a brisk pace, trying not to bump into people or accidentally slide my shoulder against a wall, which would likely knock down one of the many bulletin boards.

"He's not a jerk, though, right?" I ask. It would seem out of character for Declan's brother to be mean, but until today, I didn't even know he had a brother.

"Nah. He's one of those guys who knows everyone. Like, makes it his business to know everyone, but when you know everyone, do you really know anyone?" Camila pauses in front of the elevators. "What room was it?"

I check Declan's text. "Three seventeen."

Camila and Amelia bypass the elevators entirely, and we climb a few flights of stairs to get to the third floor, where we go down the long carpeted hall past many dorms that are hosting gatherings this evening. There are signs plastered in the halls reminding residents that it's finals week and to be quiet because people are studying, but those are mostly ignored.

We're a handful of dorm rooms away, and from this angle, I can tell that the door to the room is wide open. I let Camila and Amelia take the lead, not super confident about showing up to a person's living space this casually. I'm more used to hanging out with friends in a living room or basement, having to exchange pleasantries with their parents upon arrival, not walking right into their bedroom.

Yet Amelia nudges me ahead, since I was technically the one invited.

There are four guys standing inside the plain white walls of the mostly packed-up dorm room, past a tower of pizza boxes, exuberantly shouting over each other as they trade controllers for an ongoing video game on the mounted screen. One of them notices us standing there and nods for the others to look.

"Are we at the right room?" I ask my sister and her friend since I don't see Declan among the crowd.

"Yeah," Camila whispers back, obviously recognizing the guys inside.

"Hey, you must be our Nebraska people! Dex's friends." Who's Dex? Yet the guy with cropped dark hair and a short beard who steps forward looks similar enough to Declan that it doesn't take a leap to assume this is his sibling. He's in an oversized Eagles T-shirt that doesn't seem to mesh well with the sort-of-corporate pleated pants and nicer shoes that he's wearing, as well. Like someone's dad trying to sport an office casual look to manage this party rather than participate. He holds his arms out wide and welcoming, and he strikes me as the kind of dude who thrives on social situations no matter what, as his voice booms over the noise of the TV. "I'm Grady. My brother should be—"

"Here, sorry." Declan emerges from the common room doorway across the hall with a stack full of paper towels in his hands. The relief I feel at his presence is almost embarrassing, and I hope not too obvious on my face. "I thought I'd have to go downstairs to let you in. We didn't have plates or anything, so I was grabbing these." He smiles at me. "I didn't know you were almost here."

"Amelia's friend lives in the building," I explain, cognizant that the rest of the room has gone somewhat quiet waiting for introductions.

Declan turns around. "This is Iris, Amelia, and—"

"Camila," Grady says, giving her a charming politician smile. I almost expect him to reach out and clasp her on the shoulder. "Good to see you again."

"Hey," Camila says with an indifferent smile.

"I hear we're driving out tomorrow?" Grady asks. "I'm an all-time champ at the license plate game. Isn't that right, Dex? Watch me find three Alaska plates."

"Sure, dude," Declan says. It doesn't evade my notice that he acts a little different around his older sibling. Standing taller with his shoulders relaxed. Ever so slightly more bro-y than the nerd I'm used to rolling dice against. But in a way that makes me feel like I'm getting the full picture of who he is.

Including this nickname.

Grady motions with his palms out wide, holding a can between two fingers. I keep expecting soda to fly everywhere, but nothing spills as he gesticulates enthusiastically. "Are we thinking like ten a.m. for tomorrow?"

I do some quick mental math. If we cover nine hours each day, plus the extra time for traffic and rest stops and food, how early do we need to leave to make sure we're not driving after dark?

Also, should I explain that we don't want to drive after dark? And why?

Amelia isn't overthinking. With a friendly smirk, she says, "Could you wake up early enough for maybe . . . eight?"

"Oof." Grady puts a hand to his chest. "Let's split the difference and say nine?"

"Agreed," my sister says with a shrug.

"Can I grab you anything to drink?" Grady offers us, gesturing to the open mini fridge behind him, but Camila is already stepping back into the hallway.

"No, thanks." Amelia turns to me. "Text if you need anything."

"Yeah," I say, more confidently than I feel, as my sister disappears with her friend down the hall.

"They can't stay?" Grady asks.

"They'll be back later." I figure that's a less complicated answer.

"Cool, cool. Don't forget to grab something to eat." Grady gestures toward the pizza before stepping away to greet some more of his guests.

Declan hands me a paper towel, and I reach to take a slice, our arms brushing together as we turn toward the boxes. "Hey, little sibs, what do you think?" Declan says to me in a joking tone.

"Oh, didn't you get the memo?" I tell him. "We don't make the plans. That's an older-sibling privilege."

Grady's already at the door but turns around mid-conversation to call back to me, "Great to meet you, Iris. Dex told me a little about the board game you were working on. I'll want to pick your brain about that tomorrow."

"Oh, sure," I say, the part that jumps out at me the most being that Declan was telling his brother something about me.

I'm a little intimidated by the growing number of college students crowding this dorm, and I'm finding it tricky to tell what Declan is saying in all the noise, especially between bites of pizza. "What was that?" I ask, staring at his lips.

"Can you not hear me?" he asks, and then nods to the empty common room that's right across the hall. I lead the way, and we take the rest of our pizza over to eat on the couch.

Declan must fall into the category of people who've known me long enough to have seen my older, more visible hearing aids, but he's also someone I've never actually discussed them with. "This is better, right?" he asks.

"Yeah, it's fine," I say, which is usually my answer whether it is or not. "Thanks."

"Of course."

"We can go back whenever."

Declan shakes his head. "I'm good here. It was getting to be a lot over there."

"Your brother is quite the social butterfly," I observe, staring back across the hall as Grady is clasping hands with even more attendees.

"Like he's constantly running for office, even when there's no election in sight," Declan says.

I chuckle at his joke but then struggle to come up with another response because my biggest instinct right now is to somehow clarify that whole text situation. But better yet, I'm just going to completely ignore that Declan saw that message from Amelia. It was a simple matter of sibling teasing. He understands that. There's absolutely no reason to bring it up or to think he's even thinking about it.

He nods toward Kermit. "I've never seen you wear that sweatshirt before."

What's a Muppet if not a conversation starter? I'm grateful. "You like it? My sister stole it, but now it's been rightfully returned."

"Gotta hate it when that happens."

"Somehow I don't see you and your brother regularly swapping clothes."

He chuckles. "Nah, can't say I have that problem. But I can still empathize."

"I appreciate it."

We fall into an easy groove, chatting for a while, mostly about anticipated Rivalry character decks, until I mention that

I could've eaten another slice of pizza and Declan jumps up to grab us some more from across the hall.

When he heads back, I check my phone to see if there's any update from Amelia, but there's not. "Actually," I say, waving my phone toward Declan while he puts the pizza on the coffee table in front of the couch, "let me send you the hotel info before I forget." I forward him the address.

He nods while taking a bite, not checking his phone. "Cool. We'll put that in the GPS."

"And . . . maybe reserve it online?" I say, shrugging.

"Yeah, maybe. Or we'll book it when we get there."

"Are you sure?" I reach to eat the cold pizza, which still tastes just as good as it did when it was slightly warmer.

He searches the hotel on the map and swipes around the surrounding area, a mix of chain restaurants, gas stations, and suburban housing. "Yeah, it's in a random Indiana town. Unless there's some convention nearby or something, I'm sure there'll be rooms."

"But wouldn't you feel better knowing there's already a room waiting for you?"

"Would *you* feel better knowing there was already a room waiting for me?" There's something about his question that feels suggestive even though it wasn't meant that way, and I look down at his phone quickly.

"You have it right there. You can just book it."

"It'll be fine," he says. "I promise."

I laugh and give up. "I genuinely don't understand how you can live like this. Just hoping things will work out."

"Does stressing about things make them any easier?" he asks.

"Not really."

"So I skip that step." He's finished eating and slumped a few inches back on the couch so that we're closer to eye level as we talk.

I hold a hand over my mouth, talking through my final bite. "Then what if it backfires?"

"I'll change my plans. Go with the flow."

"I simply don't understand," I say. "It feels like a board game, though, doesn't it? I'm even dreaming in board game ideation these days."

Even though I didn't fully explain my thought, Declan knows exactly where I'm going with it. "A road trip does hit so many classic beats. Maybe it's not even about sightseeing, but more about leveling up with mundane tasks, like getting experience tokens for filling up a gas tank."

"And the tank can only take you so many spaces around the board," I say, jumping into the brainstorming without missing a beat. "Then you could have to somehow refill or get stranded." Unfortunately, the more I think about it, the less sure I am. "What's interesting or unique about it, though? How is it more compelling than just a drive-across-a-map game?"

"I'm not sure." Declan taps his fingers on the couch.

"Well, we can ponder," I say. "I'll text you if I think of something."

He smiles. "Yeah, now you can text me anytime."

Shoot, with *the* text still nagging at me, I inadvertently

mentioned texting, and now there isn't a single doubt in my mind that we're both thinking about that crush text.

I need to pivot away immediately. "How did I not know you have a brother?"

Declan raises his eyebrows. "Hey, I wasn't keeping him a secret. You never asked."

"I'm asking now!"

"I have a brother," he says, amused by his own joke.

I shake my head multiple times; it makes me dizzy. "Okay, well, tell me something else I don't know about you."

He leans back on the couch and turns his face toward me. "My middle name is Conor?"

Perhaps I should have come up with a more creative question. "Nice name."

"What about yours?"

I mirror his relaxed position. "It's pretty classic. And way overused in my family."

He tilts his chin quizzically. "I've got a couple ideas, but give me the first letter."

"M."

Exactly one second later, he says, "Hmm, let me think what other questions I have for Iris Marie Biagi."

Him getting it right on his first guess throws me off balance. "Don't go stealing my identity now."

Declan's face grows more serious, and I can sense an actual question coming my way. "What about that time you showed up crying? A few weeks ago? I wanted to make sure you were okay, but you told people you didn't want to talk about it, so I didn't want to bother you. Though you don't have to tell me if—"

"Oh." It doesn't take long to figure out what night he's talking about. A small laugh slips from my lips.

He relaxes. "It's funny?"

"I wouldn't have still gone to play Rivalry if it was tragic." Though my eyes are welling again now from the amusement of it all. "I'm almost embarrassed to tell you because it was actually nothing."

"It couldn't have been nothing?"

"I was having a bad day, but just, like, annoying-classes-level bad. On the way into Roll Again, I stubbed my toe on the curb." I chuckle at the retelling of this pointless incident, causing Declan to laugh as well. "Which was apparently the last straw? But then I walked into the store with a tear running down my cheek, and everyone was so concerned, which made me"—I wipe away the water from the corner of my eyes—"cry even more because it was all so nice? One of those days, I guess." I don't want to dwell on this ridiculousness. "But that reminds me . . . you never told me how you broke your arm?"

He starts laughing even harder than me.

"What?" I ask.

Declan reaches out and puts his hands on my shoulders. "There was also a curb involved."

Our fits of giggles have briefly garnered some attention from across the hall.

Declan sits back and gestures to himself. "Despite looking like I could be a natural skateboarder . . . I am most certainly not."

"Oh no!" I say, but can't stop laughing. "I'm sorry, it's not funny."

"It is now." Declan reaches for my arm and scribbles with his fingers across my skin as if writing something, making me catch my breath. "You signed your name in huge letters on that cast. Prime real estate all the way across."

"There was a lot of empty space. I felt bad!"

He gives a silly gasp. "Iris, I hadn't gone back to school with it yet."

"Ohhh, of course." That didn't dawn on me back then.

"The next day everyone kept asking me who you were."

"Really?" I need to know what he told people about me.

Declan bites his lip, debating if he should say exactly. "They thought I had a mystery girlfriend at another school."

My jaw drops. I was not expecting that. "Oh my gosh, why would they think that?"

"You seriously don't remember?" He opens his mouth wide, ready to tease me with a final detail. "Because you also drew a heart."

My face goes bright red. "No . . . I mean . . ." I lift my finger and trace a tiny little heart in the air, his gaze laser focused on following my motion. "A little *get well soon* one, you know?"

"Well, thank you, because it made the other eighth graders think I was cooler than I actually was."

I reach out and wrap my hands around his wrist, pulling him toward me. "You should've told me. That's hilarious."

"Hilarious because?" He averts his eyes, staring down at how I'm holding his arm.

I recoil, pulling my hands back into my own lap. This is my chance to deny the crush allegations, but maybe a denial wouldn't be entirely accurate after all?

Like somehow the total tally of my interactions with Declan has led to this one specific moment where I need to choose to deny or confess or . . .

Or what I end up saying, which is, "Because I had a fake boyfriend and didn't even know it."

He laughs, looking away. "Apparently not."

"But," I say slowly, watching him now cling to my every word while my own brain spins, "you're telling me now?"

"I thought it would be funny to mention." He's looking at me as if waiting for me to say something more concrete.

We're at a stalemate.

I can't possibly make this question any clearer, can I? I bring my hands together, laced underneath my chin. A journalist preparing to ask the most revealing question. "And is there a reason you wanted to mention it?"

He opens his mouth to say something, then closes his lips, only to try again. "Because I—"

"Iris." Amelia bounds into the common room. "You gave me a heart attack when I couldn't find you," she says, gesturing back to the dorm.

"It was loud," I say, turning over the back of the couch and away from Declan. "Are you ready to call it?" I ask her.

"Yeah, early drive tomorrow," my sister says, waving goodbye to Declan. "Good luck getting any sleep over there tonight."

He nods. "Don't worry, I'll make sure we're up and ready by nine."

"It doesn't have to be, like, exactly nine," Amelia says, trying to be more casual than she actually is. "But not too late."

Unprompted, across the hall, Grady jumps onto one of the mattresses. "Hey, I love you all, but we gotta move the party. Keep in touch and I'll catch you next year. Go Birds!"

There are a few *woot-woot*s in reply, and though it takes a few minutes, the room actually empties out. Grady walks over into the common room with a wide smile. "Early morning tomorrow," he says to Amelia.

Amelia isn't that impressed by his theatrics but gives a polite grin.

Grady points toward Amelia with an eager click of his teeth. "I'm going to set the alarm right now." He holds up his phone but accidentally clicks the calculator app first. "Whoops, just doing some quick math."

My sister gives a halfhearted laugh. Though I doubt she caught the visual gag, she could obviously pick it up from context. "Okay, see you both tomorrow," she says, giving a small wave with her lanyard of keys in hand.

I follow Amelia out the common room door, feeling Declan's gaze before I glance over my shoulder. Our eyes lock, whatever words he was about to say lost on his lips.

Chapter Eight

Last night already feels like a hazy memory. An evening plucked from the near future, if it's any indication of how I'll spend my time at college this fall. When I think too clearly about what next year could look like, it makes my stomach twist with anticipation.

Yet right now reality hits hard in the bright sunlight peeking out from the clouds as I stand in front of Franklin Hall with a cart full of my sister's stuff, waiting for Amelia to pull around with the car. Any bravery I summoned yesterday to question how I feel about Declan has already evaporated with the morning dew.

We load the suitcases into the trunk first, then shove all the garbage bags of extra stuff around them, putting the pillows in the back seat, along with our bags for tonight.

"Did you want to leave anything behind in storage for next year?" I ask, almost as an afterthought, when we look at everything squared away.

"I thought about it," Amelia says, reaching forward to re-adjust a bag so it won't get caught as she slams the trunk closed. "But I want to sort through everything at home and fly back next year with only the stuff I need. I packed way too much for this year." She turns this into preachy older sister advice. "Honestly, whatever you pack, cut it in half and only take main essentials. You'll accumulate so much stuff throughout the year. Just the free T-shirts alone . . ."

"That's months away. I haven't even thought about packing yet." I turn and glance down the road toward Delancey Hall. "What time is it?"

Amelia holds her phone up to her face. "Eight fifty-five."

I squat down alongside the car, stretching my left leg and then my right, not ready to be cooped up for nine hours on the road today. "Do you want to drive first or me?"

"I'll go first," she says through a yawn. "Should we find coffee?"

"Since when do you drink coffee?" I ask, eyes narrowed as I reach my hands toward the sky, twisting my back until it cracks.

A white SUV slowly turns in front of the dorm, pulling to a stop on the opposite side of this one-way street, with just enough space for another car to drive between our two vehicles if it needed to get by.

The passenger-side window rolls down, and from the driver's seat, an energetic Grady in a college-branded polo—looking more ready for a team-building experience on the golf course than a drive across the country—leans across his brother to shout out toward us, "We're ready to hit the road at nine!"

"I'm grabbing coffee," my sister calls out. "Want anything?"

Grady lets out a deep chuckle. "But it's already almost nine . . ."

Without missing a beat, Amelia counters, "Good thing I've still got three minutes. Anyone for coffee?"

"No, thanks," Grady says, which Declan and I echo.

"Wow, okay. I'll be right back." She quickens her step as she rounds the corner toward a coffee cart.

Declan's hair is a mess of bedhead beneath the raised hood of his sweatshirt. Grady was doubting an early morning, but Declan seems to be the one having the most difficulty being awake right now. Even so, as I stand around my car awkwardly, Declan gives a small sleepy smile and waves me over.

He pulls out a piece of paper with a brainstormed list of ideas for a road trip–inspired game. I sheepishly hold open the dozen bullet points of similar thought I'd gathered on my notes app.

"Should we actually try to put something together for the teams category?" I ask. If someone had told me a week ago that I'd want to work with Declan on a joint submission, I never would've believed it.

He hands me his notes. "We might already have it halfway figured out."

I laugh, taking a closer look at what Declan's written, but I haven't shared my own thoughts since I'm more apprehensive to outright hand him my phone again. "I think we could actually pull this off. It probably wouldn't win, but might as well try, right?"

"Exactly," he agrees.

Leaning on the open window of his SUV, I catch a gust of cinnamon and peppermint and . . . nutmeg? "Your car smells like Christmas?"

Declan sluggishly points toward the freshener tag on the air vent, then to another at the center console, and over his shoulder presumably to more in the back among the pile of duffel bags of stuff.

Grady nods, almost proud, not insulted in the least. "Mom buys them in bulk. Might as well keep that holiday spirit year-round, am I right?"

"Sure, why not?" I say, though skeptical.

Do I keep standing here until Amelia gets back? Should I go wait in the car? Declan is now on his phone, and Grady is just kind of looking at me, perhaps waiting for me to continue the conversation? Or getting a good look in the daylight at the girl his younger brother wants to spend more time with. His staring feels more like friendly curiosity than judgment, but it makes me want to vanish into thin air all the same, unsure how to make a good impression.

"Here, I've got the address," Declan says, reaching to plug his phone in to the car and leaving it on the center console.

"But you've got my playlist on, right?" Grady asks, nodding toward the radio.

Declan confirms, but he throws a sly wince in my direction. "Driver's choice."

"So, Dex says you're going to be in Indy this fall too?" Grady asks, gently tapping his fists on the steering wheel, unable to sit still.

"I will be," I say a little too loudly, swinging my arms at my side, trying to act aloof.

"That's cool. You two can drive home together for breaks and stuff," Grady says.

That seems to be what finally wakes Declan up. He turns his shoulders toward me, feeling the need to walk back the certainty of his brother's statement. "If the timing works out, with classes or whatever."

"Yeah, yeah, of course," I say, a little chilled by his sudden indifference. I must've been reading too much into our conversation last night.

Amelia walks back with a tall cup of coffee, pausing beside me. "Do you have the address?" she asks them.

The guys nod, so I say out loud, "Yeah, they've got it."

"Do you want to take the lead?" Grady asks. "I'm good either way."

"Sure," Amelia says. "We can stop about two hours in at a rest stop to switch drivers?"

"Probably a lot healthier than the long stretches we usually do," Declan tells Grady.

"Cool," I say, following Amelia to our car. I peek back over the hood to call out, "Um, just text me if we get separated." I duck back down into the car and must've missed Declan saying something else, because he sends a text.

Declan: Or if I get bored?

Iris: That's fine too!

On most drives together, Amelia and I usually save *Wicked* for later on, when we need an adrenaline boost, but she cues it up right from the start. I honestly couldn't tell you the actual plot of this musical, but I know almost every word of the soundtrack by heart, and the ones I don't know, I can vocalize some random sounds that fill in the gaps well enough.

Amelia sings in the car with a lot of confidence, the lyrics increasing her focus on the road during long driving stretches, though at some points in the song, when belting out big moments, she'll reach her hand across to grab my shoulder theatrically.

I'm glad to be the car in front, where Declan doesn't have an easy view of me singing my lungs out . . . the way I do of him each time I glance back in the side mirror. At first, he seemed to be slumped against the seat, asleep, but now he and Grady are laughing about something. When he looks forward, I tell myself to stop wondering if he's looking at me, because when I look at the cars in front of us, I can never see the people in them clearly. At the same time, I avoid looking back in his direction as we reach the end of the *Wicked* soundtrack, particularly during "As Long as You're Mine."

When "For Good" wraps up and we've still got another half hour to go until our first rest stop, Amelia asks, "Should we put on a podcast?" She puts a hand to her throat. "My voice is all scratchy after that."

"You can listen to whatever," I say. "I'll stream to my hearing aids for a bit."

It gives me a headache to listen to spoken audio over the car stereo rather than music, because I need it to be clear and direct for me to actually understand everything that's being said, which, when combined with the noise of the car and the road, is no easy feat. But through the Bluetooth on my hearing aids, it's not as much of a problem.

Also, Amelia chose a celebrity talk podcast, whereas I've got a new episode of medical mysteries I've been dying to listen to, which my sister doesn't enjoy because they're too detailed and make her queasy.

Declan: Whatcha up to?

The corners of my lips curl up. I turn to look into their car, where I find him yawning again, leaning back against his seat and looking at his phone. Waiting for a response from me? I bite my lip, trying not to look too pleased at this basic message—not that he nor my sister can see my expression right now anyway.

Iris: Listening to a podcast. What about you?

Declan: It's NPR time . . .

Iris: Ooh

Declan: He thinks he might be mentioned soon.
Well, the professor he helped with
a research project will be mentioned,
which counts apparently

Iris: Aww I hope they mention him!

Declan doesn't respond for a while, but when I look back through the mirror, I see Grady low-key fist pumping the air.

Iris: Congrats???

Declan: :gasp: are you spying on us?

Iris: Your SUV shook with joy

Declan: He's pretty proud of himself. Fair warning,
he's going to have a lot of energy when we stop

The exit ramp to the rest stop veers off the highway, bringing us to a grassy area with a small building that has bathrooms and vending machines, as well as a short walking path that loops around the building among tall trees. There are only a couple other cars here, but they're all parked close together right by the front entrance, with only one bigger truck parked farther down in the rows of empty spaces.

Grady parks a few spaces to the left of our car and immediately leaps out to do a set of jumping jacks. Amelia and I turn to look, and Declan notices her driving glasses as he climbs out of the SUV.

I expect Amelia to do the same dismissal of this as she did on campus, but she holds them in her hands as she steps into the parking space, giving me a pointed expression, like *Happy now?* and she holds them up toward the guys. "These are just my driving lenses."

Declan nods politely while Grady steps closer to ask, "Huh, I was gonna say, what are those? I've never seen anything like that before."

"They're telescopic lenses," she explains, pointing to the components at the center. "To see certain things zoomed in because of my vision loss."

"That's interesting," Declan says.

"Can I try them on?" Grady asks. "Sorry, you probably get that question all the time."

Amelia shakes her head. "Uh, I don't want to stretch them or anything."

"Then I definitely shouldn't try them on. I have been told that I have a big head," Grady says proudly. He leans forward to look at the lenses in Amelia's hands. "We should get some for Pops," he says before explaining, "Our grandpa has his trusty binoculars that he brings when he goes out for most anything."

Amelia puts them back in the case and slides them into the sunglasses compartment in the car before we head toward the restroom.

"You didn't have to do that," I tell her as we wash our hands in front of the mirror.

"We're going to be driving with them for this long, might as well rip off the Band-Aid. It was easy enough."

"Yeah, you did a good job."

She rolls her eyes. "Ooh, thank you . . ."

"Just saying."

We emerge outside again, where Grady is doing a few unsteady lunges up and down the path through the trees. Declan is around the corner at the little vending machine hut.

"Do you want any candy?" I ask Amelia.

"No, that's fine. I'll try calling Mom and Dad."

"Okay, I'll be right back."

As I step away, Grady jogs over to chat with Amelia. An old lady walks past them on her way inside the building and says something that makes them both erupt with laughter.

"What was that?" I ask, approaching Declan, curious if he overheard.

He's staring back at our siblings with an amused expression. "She said they make a very cute couple."

"Oh." I laugh, because Amelia seems to revile Grady.

Declan points to the machine. "Want to split some chocolate? A3?"

"Looks good to me."

We silently watch the machine dispense the bar, which he retrieves and hands me. "We can divide it later?"

"Sure, thanks." I wave it back in the direction of the cars.

"Well, I should, um, go see if Amelia called our parents. And maybe you should get in a lap or two . . ." I tease, gesturing toward his brother, who is now sprinting up and down the path.

At first, I doubt Declan is going to, but he shouts after Grady, "Race you!" then disappears down the path in the opposite direction, with a significant head start, but his brother wastes no time trying to catch up.

I walk over to Amelia, who's meandered down the sidewalk and is standing about a driveway's length away from the car, texting something on her phone. "Hey," I say, startling her.

"Iris?" Her eyes go wide.

"Uh, yeah?" But she isn't in a goofy mood. Now she seems genuinely afraid. "What's up?" I ask.

"If you're there . . . who's in our car?" She points to the sedan, where I realize someone is sitting in the passenger seat.

At first, I stand behind my older sister, grabbing onto her arm. There's someone in our car. Who seems to be sitting there, not really doing anything. This person must have gotten in while I was distracted at the vending machine. Except that doesn't explain *why* they're in our vehicle. They're not hiding in the back or messing around with anything.

"What's happening?" Amelia asks me, trying to keep her voice level but obviously shaken.

"I'll walk closer," I say in a hush.

"No, wait," she says.

Grady and Declan head over to us at a normal but cautious gait, still breathing heavily from their impromptu race. "Everything all right?" Grady asks. Amelia flicks her finger quickly toward the lot. It only takes them a second to follow our gazes and discover the problem. "Is that someone in your car?"

"Yeah," Amelia whispers, even though there's no one else in earshot.

"It's fine," I insist, though not feeling very fine about it at all. "It's not like they're in the driver's seat. I'll go walk by and check it out."

"No," Amelia says, but seems to be running calculations in her head and follows up with, "Not too close."

"Sure." I take a deep breath and walk down the sidewalk, turning to move perpendicular to the row of parked cars, with a not-so-discreet turn of my head to stare directly through the windshields. But then I realize the mistake and shuffle back to my sister, shoulders relaxed.

"Okay, you're never going to believe it," I say, building suspense.

Declan looks toward the lot and seems to come to the same conclusion before I announce it. "Ah, I see it."

"What?" Amelia asks, eyes wide.

I clasp my hands together. "That's not our car."

In the row of parked vehicles, our silver sedan with Nebraska license plates sits right between the white SUV and another silver car, the exact same make and model, also with Nebraska plates.

She scrunches up her face. "Are you sure?"

"Yep." I gently nudge her arm to tilt her so that she's facing the vehicle one parking space over. "That one is."

"You're sure?" she repeats.

"Yep," I say, reaching out my hands to take the keys from her. I hit the unlock button, and our empty car to the right lights up. "We're all good."

But Amelia's face remains contorted. "I was sure."

"It's fine," I try to reassure her.

"Yeah, we all thought the same. Easy mistake to make," Grady says, hand on her shoulder, which Amelia doesn't shrug away from, though she cringes at the word *mistake*. Not something my sister is fond of. "You know what." Grady's good at trying to recalibrate a drop in energy. "Let's switch things up for the next stretch. Do we want to do some passenger swapping here?"

"What? Like go in different cars?" I ask, instinctively glancing toward Declan.

I'm pleased to find him looking my way as well. "That sounds fun," he says.

Amelia is staring off into the distance, still shaken—and I'm not sure whether it's from the initial fear of someone having gotten into our car or from having gotten concerned about something that turned out to not be a problem at all. But really, she shouldn't feel too bad; it wasn't an impossible mistake to make, but I'm sure she's still stuck feeling a certain way about it.

My sister crosses her arms and speaks to Grady. "But you and I just drove. If those two pair up, one of us has to drive again."

"Really, I'm good to drive another stretch," Grady says to Amelia, bouncing on his heels like he's warming up for sports practice. "All right, perfect. So I'll go with Lee, and Iris can drive with Dex?"

"Works for me!" Declan says.

"Sure," I agree before realizing that Amelia is shooting daggers my way.

My sister turns to Grady, accepting her fate, but not going down without a fight. "It's Amelia," she corrects.

Grady isn't put off. "I get it. Nicknames have to be earned. I'll get there."

She crosses her arms. "Let's just drive to the next stop. I'm keeping my music on."

I don't move from where I'm standing. Should I offer to just stick with Amelia? She seems better by the second, however, and driving home with the guys was her idea, after all. She can't be too upset about getting stuck with Grady for a bit.

Declan grabs the keys from his brother and gestures to the SUV. "You good, Iris?"

"Oh, sure, yeah." I reach into the car and grab my bag, which is when I remember I'm still holding this chocolate bar. "Easier to split this."

"Exactly." But his brow is furrowed. It makes me question the change of seating arrangements. It'll be nice to have time to brainstorm on the drive with Declan, but I was supposed to be spending time with my sister this week.

Chapter Nine

Declan approaches the SUV first to clear out the side door, tossing some snack trash into the nearby garbage can. With the day no longer early morning cool, he takes off his sweatshirt, and I walk past, climbing into the passenger seat, pretending not to notice his tee underneath slide up as he does so. He takes the driver's seat and tosses the sweatshirt in the back on his brother's bags.

"We can roll the windows down if the scent gets to be too much," Declan offers, lowering the blast of air-conditioning and repositioning one of the air fresheners that had started to fall off the vent. He fastens his seat belt and watches as I click into the passenger seat.

"It's all right. It smells nice." I take a deep breath and sniff.

It's comfortable, and I feel right at home, not minding that the pine scent is at odds with the warm weather.

"Good. I mostly don't want you catching a whiff of the laundry bags," Declan teases.

"It makes me feel like we should wear mittens and drink hot chocolate." I almost add *and cuddle by the fireplace* but stop myself just in time, though I can't prevent myself from recalling when Declan stood in the doorway on a game night this past winter, knocking snow from his boots and absentmindedly pulling off his wool hat, nose red from the cold.

"At least we have chocolate," he says. "Want to open it?"

I fumble with tearing the plastic, having to turn the bar to the other side, while looking out the window. Grady is adjusting the mirrors in our car as Amelia messes with the music. What I'd give to be a fly on the wall in that car for the next two hours.

"I'm not sure our siblings get along," I say.

Declan laughs. "Grady can take some getting used to."

"At least we don't have to worry about them dating or something. That would be weird."

"Would it?" Declan isn't perturbed by my statement. He holds out a hand, and I drop a few squares of chocolate as he nods toward the glove compartment. "There's probably some napkins in there."

"Do we really need napkins?" I ask.

"I mean . . ." He arches an eyebrow. "I may be experiencing some minor trauma from you tearing me a new one about smudgy fingers near your *precious* card deck."

Oh shit, he remembers that.

I didn't think I'd made that big of a deal about it, but obviously it was enough to make a lasting impression. Hopefully, I wasn't *that* obnoxious about it, but I still cringe at the prospect of my gorgeous character cards covered in grimy candy residue, so I stand by my reaction.

I tilt my head back and laugh. "No, you can't hold that one against me. Your hands were like—" He holds up the chocolate, which is already starting to melt in his palm. "Like that!"

He licks his palm clean. "What were you saying about our siblings dating?"

Grady pulls out of the spot and drives down the rest stop ramp slowly, waiting for Declan and me to start merging back into traffic. Declan holds out his hand until I find him a napkin, then turns on the ignition and follows the car onto the highway.

"That it seems incredibly unlikely." I don't understand why there's some part of me that needs reassurance about this. "She really seemed to hate that he was calling her by her nickname already."

Declan's amused by my logic and not the least bit unsettled. "If there's one thing my brother loves, it's a nickname."

"Yeah, Dex," I tease.

"Actually, most people call me that."

That's earth-shattering information.

My jaw drops. "What?"

"Like, at school. Probably because they always heard my brother calling me that," he explains. I lean over the center and tap Declan's arm several times, which he ignores, though his smile grows, until he finally relents to ask, "Can I help you?"

I keep my fingers resting against his skin. "Have I been calling you by the wrong name?"

He glances from the road to my baffled expression. "I like that you call me Declan. Not a lot of people do."

"Really?" My concern melts away into a feeling of being special, something a little bit unique. Like a reverse nickname.

"Mostly just some family, and you guys at Roll Again." Declan nods confidently, then suddenly goes shy when he glances down to my hand still on his arm, and he returns to the initial subject as I pull away. "But, yeah, I'm glad our siblings are getting along well enough for this drive. It's a fun time."

"Of course," I agree.

He thinks for a second, then adds, "But them dating seems . . . highly unlikely."

I laugh. "Exactly."

It's so obvious that Amelia finds his brother mildly irritating to say the least. But hold on—is Declan implying that Grady wouldn't be interested in my sister?

Amelia is great. Funny, smart, and a total catch. Any guy would be so *lucky* to catch her interest. I remember Grady's curiosity about her driving glasses earlier, and my immediate reaction here is to get super defensive.

"Is it because my sister—"

"What? No, nothing against your sister," Declan is quick to reassure, turning to make eye contact once more. "I didn't mean to make it seem like that. It's just Grady has never seemed interested in dating, well, *anyone*."

"Oh," I say, realization washing over me. "I get that."

"So, combined with the fact that they don't really seem to like each other much to begin with, my guess is that you really don't need to worry about them getting together like that."

He's making it seem like this is some huge unfounded concern of mine.

"Why would I be worried?" I ask.

"You *just* said it would be weird."

I break off another piece of chocolate, but when I go to give it to him, he keeps his hands on the wheel and opens his mouth. I roll my eyes and toss it onto his tongue. "Why would it be weird?"

His face is blank. "I . . . can't think of any reason."

"Exactly." I take the final piece of chocolate for myself to finish the bar, folding the candy wrapper in half several times and sliding it into the cupholder to dispose of later.

Yet Declan looks at me out of the side of his eye, a smile curling up on his lips. "But if you think of a reason, let me know."

"Or if *you* think of anything," I counter, worried we're trapped in an endless game of chicken, but I'm not brave enough to be the one to make a move here. I like how things have been going between us these last couple days and don't want to do anything that could jeopardize that.

The highway divides, and he merges to the left to follow our siblings and the GPS. Should we play some music? It's his car. I'll let him take the lead on that, at least.

Declan chooses to keep making conversation. "What do you have going on the rest of this summer?"

"Um, attending lots of graduation parties." I cross my legs on the seat and lean against the headrest. The seat belt is tight as I turn to face him, so I hold it loosely in my hands to keep it from stabbing me in the neck. "Hanging with Amelia before she ditches me for Europe, this big impressive study abroad program she'll be at for three months. Picking up shifts at my friend Peyton's family restaurant."

"I know Peyton," Declan reminds me.

"I can't believe I forgot for a second that you also know Peyton. And obviously, going to play Rivalry," I add with a laugh.

"You'll need to get in as many matches as possible to improve your stats."

"What about you?"

He eases on the brake as some car weaves through traffic going ninety. "Well, work shifts and game nights at Roll Again. Then Grady likes to drag me along to canvass for certain progressive issues whenever they need an extra guy, but he's going to be busy this summer with an internship. Roy and I like to go fishing at his dad's place . . . You know Roy," he teases me.

Roy is the short guy with big glasses, whom I've never seen talk much except in impassioned bursts about new game releases. "I know him, but I didn't realize you two were that close."

"Yeah, he's a good guy." Declan taps the steering wheel.

"It's strange, I don't think Roy and I have played against each other lately."

"Oh, really?" Declan goes quiet, a flush rising on his cheeks. "I hadn't noticed."

Anticipation courses through me, because I have a sneaking suspicion of where this is going. "What'd you do?"

"His parents are big on curfew for school nights. And you were running late sometimes—well, most times—this year. If he was your assigned partner and you weren't there right at the start when tables were assigned, we'd trade."

"You arranged it 'cause you wanted to play against *me*." I enjoy watching him squirm in his seat.

"I wanted Roy to get home before curfew," he says, struggling to keep a straight face. "If he got grounded, we couldn't go fishing."

"That makes sense." The smile is still plastered to my face.

"And, um, what else?" He scratches his elbow, glancing back out the rearview mirror. "This summer we're selling the house, so that will take a lot of work, getting everything sorted through and packed up, though a lot of stuff is probably going to sit in storage for a while until it all gets figured out."

I panic that he could be going somewhere far away and I'll never see him again, that this new familiarity with Declan could slip through my fingers as easily as it started these last few days—all before I remember that we've already established we're going to the same college.

"Why are you moving?"

"Well, my parents are. Basically, it's time to get out of that house. I'm not sure where they'll end up."

I wish he'd give a few more details, but I don't want to pry. "Wow, that's open-ended."

"It's strange moving out before leaving for college. Like, I'll never be able to revisit that part of my childhood again. My life will always be divided into a before and after." He presses his lips together, puffing out his cheeks with air. "I have no idea where I'll spend the holiday breaks. I can table that problem until Thanksgiving."

"That's a lot of change at once," I agree.

"Yeah . . . I'll wait and see how it goes."

"That does seem to be your preferred approach to life."

He shrugs. "Sometimes it's the best choice, all things considered."

"So, like, are your parents going to move really far away?"

"Something like that." He doesn't clarify, and I decide not to press.

"Well, I guess you could be invited to Thanksgiving at my place, if you don't have other plans."

"Really?" Declan stares right at me with an intrigued smile that makes my heart burst.

"Watch the road!" I say, waving away his gaze when I can no longer bear it. "It's like your brother said earlier: I'll need someone to split the drive back home for breaks," I tease. "It's only fair that that deal come with some turkey."

•••••

At lunchtime we stop at this quirky little 1950s diner that Amelia found while searching for dining options at our upcoming exits. It's out of place among the typical gas stations and golden arches that seem to be at every single highway intersection. Even among all this empty space, the parking lot is a tight squeeze, as though not paved for the size of modern vehicles. Declan has to pull the SUV through into a narrow spot near the dumpsters.

Inside, we take a seat at an empty booth with blue-and-red swirl posts while a few truckers eat at the counter next to dishes of pie slices. There's a QR code on a folded piece of cardstock in the center of the table, but a middle-aged waitress walks over and gestures for us to ignore that, plopping down wide plastic-covered menus and filling four cups of water. "Give me a shout when you know what you want," she says, returning behind the counter.

Grady barely consults the menu before he's found exactly what he wants. "Club sandwich," he says, nodding toward Declan.

Declan shrugs. "I think I'll do a burger."

Amelia pulls out her phone to use the magnifying app, scanning it over the menu's text. I take my time, as well, even though I've already zoned in on the French toast. "You like grilled cheese," I suggest.

Her interest is piqued. "They have that?" She scans over the bottom left-hand corner and finds it. "I'll get that."

"Excuse me!" Grady waves his arms, not shouting, per se, but his voice easily carries. "We're ready whenever you are."

The waitress returns and takes our order. Meanwhile, another family gets up from their table, getting ready to leave, and the girl about our age pauses in front of us on her way back from the bathroom, looking right at Amelia.

"Hey," the girl says, excited to see my sister. "What are you doing here?"

Amelia falters, struggling to recognize her.

"I'm Iris," I say, jumping in. "How do you know my sister?"

"Eden," she introduces herself with even more enthusiasm. "We sat next to each other in algebra last year. Amazing to see you!" she says to Amelia. "You look so good. Did you dye your hair?" Before my sister can answer, Eden continues. "I gotta catch up with the others, but wow, amazing to see you."

"Yes, so great!" Amelia says, but there's something off about her response. She slides a hand out on the table as though telling us to hold our reaction until Eden and her family have left. "Um . . ."

"What?" I ask.

She glances toward the door to make sure the girl is gone, then bursts out laughing. "I did *not* know that person at all."

"Wait, really?" I cackle. "I just assumed you couldn't recognize them here."

"Nope," she continues. "I don't know anyone named Eden. Didn't take algebra last year. Definitely didn't dye my hair."

"I thought there was something off," I say.

"I know. I was trying to figure out the voice, like maybe it was someone from high school but they meant to say a few years ago instead of last year, but nope. No idea who that person was. And I wasn't going to correct her."

Declan and Grady seem confused, but they chuckle along and don't ask for clarification about the situation, which Amelia doesn't offer, so it's not my place to do so. My sister so often has to play along with a conversation, unable to recognize someone she *actually knows*, that it's kind of funny to have done the same with a case of mistaken identity. I didn't know anything was off until Amelia revealed that she'd put the pieces together yet was still going along with the conversation as if nothing was amiss.

It makes me curious how Amelia fares at college, with something as regular an occurrence as walking across the quad. When someone passes by and says hello, how often does she actually know who's speaking to her? Maybe she can recognize them by a backpack or bright pair of shoes they wear on a regular basis, but otherwise I'd have to guess that it could often feel like wading through a sea of vaguely familiar strangers.

How do you explain that something as off-putting as that can also make for an amusing situation like this one at the diner? I doubt Declan and Grady would fully understand why we found this funny.

Anyway, our food arrives at the table, which changes the subject easily enough.

"Did you text Dad back?" Amelia asks as she peels apart her grilled cheese slices.

"No, not yet." I reply in the family chat, letting our parents know where we've stopped.

I hold up my phone to take a picture of our meals to send to them, but Declan slides a peace sign into view. I smile and shake my head, quickly taking a full candid photo of him and his brother across from us in this booth before taking a selfie of all four of us and then another food picture—without a boy's hands—to send to my parents.

Did Amelia tell them that we're caravaning? Because I haven't.

"How do we look?" Grady asks when I'm still looking at a picture on my phone, presumably thinking it's the group selfie, but my eyes are stuck on the first image of Declan.

"Oh, it was fine," I say. "Just responding to a text."

Is this picture . . . cute?

Declan has such a casual, goofy look on his face. It's better than any of those pictures Peyton found from the game shop. I might as well send this to the group chat, right?

Peyton and Elizabeth *immediately* reply to my text.

Peyton: Look at you all romantic in a diner!!!

Elizabeth: That's him?? He's even cuter than I thought. Maybe I should play board games

Peyton: Damn, that's not the Declan I remember from a week ago.

I'm glued to my phone, heart racing as I respond, desperate for them to continue to reply right away so I can be absolutely positive I didn't somehow send the text to the wrong person, even though I'm staring at this chat right now.

Iris: I might be very mistaken, but I think he maybe likes me?

Peyton: Obviously

Iris: Not obviously!!

Declan nudges my foot underneath the table, and I nearly drop my phone on the floor. "Are you going to eat?" he asks.

I'd forgotten about my French toast. It still looks delicious and warm, waiting for me to pour syrup all over it. "Yeah, yeah. One second, just texting my parents."

Amelia raises her eyebrows, since her phone and the family chat hasn't been receiving any of the texts I've been sending.

Then, to my surprise, Amelia suggests, "I feel like we should play a game or something."

"Like the picnic game?" I ask.

"I don't know that one," she says. The guys shake their heads.

I smile, shoving my phone away and taking a quick bite of my meal while thinking for a second to set the category for our game. "Oh, it's easy. I'm going on a picnic, and I'll bring corn." The others look at me blankly. "Okay, Lee, now you say that you're going on a picnic and what you'll bring. And I'll tell you if you can go; otherwise you have to keep guessing."

She takes another bite of her melty grilled cheese. "All right, well, I'm going on a picnic, and I'll bring pizza."

I shake my head. "Nope, sorry, you can't come."

"Why not?" she asks.

"It has to fit a certain requirement," I explain, chopping another piece of my French toast to have a bite ready to eat. "So keep guessing!"

"What about an empanada?" Grady asks.

Declan points toward his brother. "You gotta say the whole phrase." He turns toward me. "Right?"

"Yeah, that's how I've always played it."

"Okay," Grady says, and proceeds to repeat his request in full.

I shake my head again, glancing out the diner window at another car arriving in the parking lot. "Sorry, you can't."

Declan thinks for a second, grabbing a napkin to dry his fingers from the burger grease before taking a drink of his soda. "I'm going on a picnic, and I'll bring rice."

I give a wide grin. "Yes, you can come!"

Declan narrows his eyes in surprise. "Really? But why?"

With a playful shrug, I turn back to my sister, who says, "I'm going on a picnic, and I'll bring chips."

"Nope!" I give a hint: "You can bring *a* chip but not chips."

Grady tries again. "I'm going on a picnic, and I'll bring *a* potato."

"Sorry!"

I worry for a second that Grady might be the type to get frustrated with this game, and that would really ruin the fun vibes we've got going here, but he gives a good-natured grin and jokes, "You know, I might start to take this personally."

"Oh," Declan says, his face lighting up. "I get it now."

"You think?" I say, shaking my head as I eat another bite.

"I'm going on a picnic . . ." Declan looks me right in the eye, pausing for effect, before saying, "and I'll bring Iris."

My heart skips a beat. "Cute." I shake my head and blush. "But, yes, you can."

"Really?" Amelia asks. "I'm going on a picnic, and I'll bring Iris?"

"Eek, sorry, you can't copy someone else's answer," I tease.

Amelia groans, slumping back in the booth. "Ugh, can I bring Grady, then, I guess?"

"No," I say, and Amelia gives a loud exhale of transparent relief.

Grady places a hand over his chest. "But I love picnics."

"Okay, so far, we can bring corn, rice, and"—I shake my head at having to refer to myself in the third person—"Iris."

Amelia leans forward. "I get it! I'm going on a picnic, and I'll bring the moon."

"Aww, that's pretty," I say. "Yes, you can bring the moon."

Grady doubles over laughing. "Can I bring the sun?"

"Nah, dude." Declan takes the opportunity to decline his brother this time for me. "You can't bring the sun."

Grady scratches his chin. "The stars?"

Declan takes another bite of his burger, placing his hand over his mouth to speak while chewing. "Don't reach for so many."

"*A* star?" Grady asks, triumphantly holding up the rest of his sandwich, lettuce slipping out onto the plate.

We all cheer.

Grady scrunches up his face as he licks his fingers clean. "Oh, four-letter words?"

Declan nods and prompts him, "So, what are you going to bring?"

Grady smiles at Amelia with a mischievous glint. "I'm going on a picnic, and I'll bring a crow."

My sister's face scrunches up, fearful and a touch repulsed, throwing Grady a look that suggests this was something they discussed in the car earlier today. "Birds do not need to crash our picnic."

"Not *birds*, plural," Grady says with a joking smirk, for some reason knowing exactly the effect this will have on Amelia. "Just one crow."

Chapter Ten

After lunch, Amelia and I congregate in the little diner restroom. While taking turns washing our hands in the small white sink, I say, "I'm good to drive for a bit now."

My sister nods, then dries her hands beneath the noisy air dryer, holding the thought until the sound stops. "Oh. It's my turn to drive again now too."

We pause, both realizing we should probably have a game plan before leaving this bathroom. "I could drive with Grady," I suggest.

Amelia stares at me, not exactly thrilled with us having to choose what to do right now with the situation we've found ourselves in. She sighs and rolls her eyes, ever the martyr. "No, it's fine, we can stay in the same cars."

I take a step backward toward the door, happy with this result even if she isn't. "Are you sure?"

She waves her hand. "Yeah, you and Declan probably want to keep flirting and talking about board games anyway." She shakes her head as if thinking *The things I do for my sister.* "You owe me."

I don't like this approach. I didn't ask her to do this. "Hey, I've said a million times this drive back home was supposed to be just the two of us."

"It's fine, really."

Amelia pushes past me and out the bathroom door, where I spot Declan and Grady through the window already waiting for us outside. "They're by the cars," I tell my sister, and she leads the way out the front entrance.

It seems like the guys must've been having a similar discussion. "I can drive again," Declan offers.

"It's all right," I say, stepping up toward the SUV. "Amelia and I already planned to drive next."

Grady eagerly turns toward Amelia. "Does that mean you want to try the podcast I was telling you about? There's a recent interview with that California congressperson I met. Their PR staffer has been doing some incredible work. I could probably connect you."

There's a glimmer to my sister's expression that I can't quite read. Not impressed, but not annoyed, either. Perhaps plain amusement? Yet she slides her weight to one hip and counters, "That's not exactly the type of work I want to do with my communications degree."

"Hey, it's all networking," Grady says.

Amelia reaches into her bag for the sedan's keys. "You could also just take a nap."

"Nah." Grady walks around to the other side of our car, voice louder as he moves farther away from the group. "Passenger is supposed to entertain the driver on a road trip."

"Except I'm more likely to fall asleep listening to you talk than listening to you snore," Amelia says, waving goodbye to Declan and me as she opens the driver's side door.

"Fair enough," Grady agrees.

It's nice and cool, with an overcast sky, which will make for good visibility on the road this afternoon, without the sun shining harshly in our eyeline. Since we're only really doing essential stops for food and gas, we're making good time to get to the hotel tonight, though it's likely we'll be doing some driving after dark.

With our siblings back in the sedan, Declan leads the way over to the SUV. He holds the driver's side door open for me to squeeze in since this was such a narrow parking job.

Scrunching up my nose at the unpleasant aroma, I say, "You basically parked in the dumpster."

"You were there. You saw what I was working with. It was the only spot available." He gently closes the door and walks around to the other side, settling into the seat beside me. "You good?"

I have to adjust the seat and the mirrors and the steering wheel, and it feels daunting. "Huh. I've never driven a car this big before. Actually, the only car I've ever driven is that one." I point to the sedan across the parking lot, where Amelia is reaching into the back seat to dig for something from her stuff.

"It's really not that different."

"Yeah, yeah. But, wow, really puts it into perspective what

drivers are seeing when you walk through a crosswalk."

"This isn't even that big compared to a lot of trucks."

"You're right. All the more terrifying." I adjust the mirrors one more time before I shift into drive and press my foot on the gas, accidentally lurching forward too quickly, right into the post of the rectangular metal parking lot sign with faded text about towing noncustomer vehicles that is two feet in front of us.

I slam on the brakes, which sends the SUV rocking back and forth.

"Shit." I take a deep, steadying breath.

Declan lets out a nervous chuckle. "What are you, blind?" he playfully teases as I reverse and right course.

It was a little love tap to the signpost, with no obvious reason to get out to try to inspect for damage to the SUV, so it's objectively amusing that I drove right into this sign.

Yet, when I don't say anything, Declan continues joking in a lighthearted fashion. "What are we going to do with you? You already can't hear."

I let out a "ha," my tone hollow, knowing for a fact that he doesn't realize he's just stabbed me right through my biggest insecurity.

Now what am I supposed to do? Get angry about a joke?

I stare straight ahead, driving incredibly slowly as I navigate out of the parking lot. It does take some adjustment to operate a different vehicle. "Sorry about that. Just need a second to get used to driving this. The way you parked, that was almost impossible to avoid."

"Yeah. . . it was a really bad parking job on my part," he admits.

I exhale, relieved to hear him say it wasn't completely my mistake, but my fingers are still wrapped tight around the steering wheel, tension in my shoulders. "I knew it was *your* fault."

My words must've come out harsher than I intended, because Declan is quick to add, "I'm just teasing."

"Yeah, I'm joking too." But I'm drained of enthusiasm for chatting. "Can you put on some music?"

Declan is eager to fix the mood somehow. "Sure, what do you want to listen to?"

"Whatever." I'm having a difficult time disguising how I'm feeling.

Mostly because I don't know *what* I'm feeling.

It was a funny accident. He made a joke most people would make, and have made often, and most people would probably find it funny. It's not the first time I've heard this, and it won't be the last. It's all funny, sure. Lightly hitting the sign *was* unexpected and therefore sort of funny.

Right? *Funny?*

Okay, this is clearly grating on me. I need to get over it already.

I drive through the intersection and to the on-ramp, following my sister onto the highway, staring straight ahead, trying to keep my expression neutral. He said it as a joke, and I know it was a joke, and I'm not even that offended by it. Not really. Why would I be?

The problem is that there's often truth hidden within a joke, and this incident has revealed that Declan would think differently about me if I also couldn't see.

If my 25 percent odds play out.

Not only will I have to worry about readjusting to the world, I'll have to worry about the rest of the world readjusting to me.

"Do you like this song?" Declan asks, though I don't recognize it over the noise of the car on the highway and can't discern the lyrics. Do I tell him that I can't even hear the song he's playing right now? I grit my teeth and stare at the road ahead, willing myself to keep it together.

To not make a big deal out of *nothing*.

"Yeah." I nod along to the music, which seems to placate him.

"I'll queue up some more," he says before singing some of the lyrics out loud to me with a goofy puppy dog look in his eyes, having no idea that right now I'm in crisis.

Declan is sweet and silly and caring. I glance over with a soft, sad smile, one that he returns tenfold, still happily bopping along to this pop hit. All this time with Declan, I've been thinking about the potential of him liking me. But maybe potential is all this will ever be, because, unfortunately, real life has a tendency to fall short.

Even if he likes me now, he's just admitted he might not like me *then*.

•••••

After another song or two, Declan stops singing along, and we pass the next half hour without talking anymore. Every minute that ticks by, negative thoughts burrow deeper into my brain, while the sights outside the window remain the exact same. Cornfields stretching on for miles against the wide-open, cloudy blue sky.

Perhaps it's soybeans, actually.

Because it's only May, the crops have yet to grow into tall, towering stalks, and they're hard to make out. With my incredibly limited agricultural knowledge, I have no idea what's in those fields. A vast sea of the unknown. It makes perfect sense why that's location fodder for horror.

It makes me picture a board game where you have to outrun a mouse through a corn maze.

Darn, I was trying my best to distract myself.

But board games take me right back to the boy sitting in the seat next to me.

"Declan?" I say, still without taking my eyes off the road.

His voice is warm and familiar, happy to be chatting again after some quiet time. "Iris?"

"There's something I need to tell you."

"Yeah?" he asks.

I brave a glance and discover there's a smile curling up on his lips, but it dissipates when he notices that my knuckles are tightly gripping the steering wheel.

"Is everything okay?" he asks.

His words from earlier still echo in my mind. *What are we going to do with you?*

Declan straightens his back, turning to face me. "You're making me nervous."

"No, don't be nervous." I wave my hand, unsure how to set the stage for this. Either I casually drop the information like it's nothing or it somehow becomes a big sob story and the conversation will get away from me.

It hits me all at once why Amelia isn't forthcoming with this information.

There's no great way to deliver it.

"Um," I say, my voice faltering. Declan reaches over and puts a hand on my arm, but I shrug him away. "No, really, um." I'm glad to be behind the wheel rather than having to look at him right now. "You know those glasses Amelia wears while driving?"

"Yeah?"

His voice is level, concerned. I can feel him getting ahead of what I'm about to say; it's clear that he's figured out where I'm going with this but is holding back until I deliver more information.

"She doesn't really talk about it, so I don't know exactly what to say here, but long story short, the condition with her eyes is genetic." I fumble with the explanation. I've gone through a script in my brain a million times, how I would explain this to someone, but here in the moment, none of it is coming out as smoothly as I'd hoped.

I glance at Declan, who is watching me intently. His concerned eyes narrow, then go wide, and his jaw goes slack. The pieces fitting into place. The reason for my big reaction to a seemingly innocuous joke. I focus back on the road.

"Basically, there's a one-in-four chance that I'll also be blind, like my sister, but for me, it would be in addition to already being deaf. In ways that will each continue to progress over my lifetime."

Declan reaches out to squeeze my arm. "I'm—I didn't know."

"This feels way too weird and somber." I wish we weren't stuck in a car right now so that I could pace around the floor. "Like, I'm *fine*. Right now it's mostly just a trippy mind game," I say, devolving into laughter, a different kind of tragic joke that somehow seems ridiculous.

His face lightens. "I don't know if you'd want to hear an apology, but can I say that I'm sorry I don't really know what reaction to give you right now?"

"Exactly!" My voice grows louder and more delirious, like this is the most hilarious thing in the world. "Like, what are you supposed to say to that?"

He shakes his head, eyebrows raised and eyes wide, with a matching grin. "I have no idea."

"But that's just it. I don't want you to feel like you can't talk normally around me. I'm not trying to tell you what you can or can't say. It's just—that comment hurt, and it hit me deeper than I thought it could. Like, if this happens, it happens, and my life continues on; I'll just have more shit to figure out, but that's life, isn't it?"

"True." He lets me continue since I show no sign of slowing down the thoughts pouring out of my mouth.

"And honestly, I love making deaf or blind jokes—Amelia and I do it all the time—they can be objectively super funny, but . . ."

I take a moment to figure out how to phrase the nuance. "But it depends on the context and situation. Like, the point of the joke is the circumstance we have to deal with, not, well, *me*."

"And I really, really didn't mean anything like that," he says. "I promise."

"Declan, I know." I keep my tone light and reach over toward him, and he grabs my hand. "But right now I don't know what my life is going to look like, and it's sometimes too much for my brain to handle. Like, the anticipation and uncertainty feel worse than the actual outcome sometimes."

"I get that." He squeezes my fingers. I take a deep breath, glad to stop talking. I said what I needed to say, but I only feel partial relief.

It distracts me from the current reality that Declan and I are holding hands. Extra confusing. I pull away from his grasp and put both of my hands back on the wheel.

"I can tell you one thing for sure," he says, brushing back his hair, suddenly bashful.

"Oh, really?" I look at him out of the corner of my eye doubtfully.

"That none of that changes the way I think about you."

I smile, realizing I'm the one giving a pitiful expression. "That's easy to say now."

He leans back. "Iris, why would any of that change how I feel about you?"

"Because other people—"

"I'm not other people." Declan says this so earnestly that I can't find a response. Then, with a cocky sort of confidence, he adds, "For a second, I thought you wanted to talk about that text."

Does this stretch of road have more potholes than the rest of the journey so far? Because I'm finding every indent of the pavement *fascinating*. "What text?"

"The one I saw on your phone yesterday." No further implications about what the question at the core of his statement is, however.

That feels like way longer ago. "That was only yesterday?" I ask.

Declan nods, serious. "I thought that was maybe something we should also discuss?"

I let out a short nervous laugh.

"I can't believe my sister sent that. She teases me all the time. I never know what she's going to say." My heart is beating so loudly I can't hear my own thoughts. "And I definitely didn't guess what she had texted or I would've checked my phone before handing it to you. I was just trying to ignore it, but you want to talk about it, probably because you've been thinking that I have some big secret crush on you. I'm sorry if that's made anything uncomfortable."

I move over to the right lane, driving slowly, then turn my shoulders ever so slightly so that Declan and I briefly stare each other down, waiting for someone to make the next move. The way we've done across the table hundreds of times. Yet this tension is charged in a way I never expected.

"You think I've been thinking that?" he asks.

We're stuck at a stalemate, again.

I sigh and admit, "Declan, I have no idea what you've been thinking."

He arches an eyebrow. "Really?"

"No." I shake my head, trying to overplay my confidence. "But I suppose we can clear things up and say that *no*, I don't have a crush on you."

"I see," he says, nodding, taking in my response. I know I'm giving off mixed signals. "Because it has been a little awkward."

"Right," I say, doubling down on laughter again, trying to disguise how my brain is reeling. I'm not sure what I expected him to say, but he seems relieved by my lack of an admission, and it's more of a letdown than I'd care to admit to myself. "Sorry about that. The last thing either of us needs is some random crush when we're about to go off to college and meet a million new people."

"Exactly," he mumbles. "However, those are some odds I feel very confident stating."

"What?"

"That there's a zero-percent chance of one of those people being another you."

"Or you," I add, breathless, feeling my very real crush squeezing the air out of my lungs. "Good thing we're friends, then, isn't it?"

Chapter Eleven

For our final rest stop of the day, with the hotel only an hour and a half away from this gas station, we refill the tanks and I rejoin Amelia in our car, offering to drive the next stretch. The only other thing at this off-ramp is the golden arches, so Grady walks into the adjoining parking lot to grab some burgers for the road, but Amelia and I are fine to dig into our shared snack stash.

Though it's not too exciting driving with my sister again, because Amelia falls asleep almost immediately as we pull back onto the highway, leaning against the headrest with her mouth wide open and drool dribbling down her chin.

The road stretches ahead, miles and miles of sameness where the view has truly only been changed by the passage of time, the sun now disappearing behind the tree line and a jarring ultra-religious billboard.

We meant to keep our travel during the daylight, but this mid-May sun will be fully set by eight, and our estimated arrival time at the hotel is 8:43 p.m. The remaining light keeps dimming until it's very dark.

In the distance, there are red lights, high in the sky, flashing in sync.

My eyes have adjusted to the darkness, but on the vast horizon, beyond the glow of nearby traffic, I can't detect the source of this eerie sight. It's so out of place. Daunting and widespread, like some sort of alien invasion.

"Whoa," I say. "Uh, Lee?"

My sister mumbles something but doesn't open her eyes.

Even as we're flying down the road at seventy miles per hour, the lights are still all encompassing, but now there are some closer, and I can truly get a sense of their height.

Then I remember exactly what they are: safety lights to alert airplanes to the windmills.

That doesn't make this scene any less fascinating. They're so bright and flashing in such rhythm. Maybe this is the unique angle that a road trip game would require.

Aliens.

I'm almost sad when we pass the last of the windmills and the light show that's kept me company for a long stretch of road.

Off the highway, it's another seven minutes until we arrive at the hotel. A streetlamp illuminates the parking lot, which isn't crowded but not empty, either, making it unclear for sure if there'll be rooms available.

I park the car and nudge Amelia awake, lifting the collar of her shirt to wipe her chin. In a silly, creepy voice, I say, "You look pretty when you sleep."

Her eyes blink open as she swats me away. "We're here?"

"Yeah."

I jump out of the car and stretch. Despite it being evening, it's warmer than I expected outside, since we've been blasting the air-conditioning. I try to prepare myself for fake pleasantries when I see Declan, tamping down the confusing emotions, but the smile that sprouts on my face at the sight of him is still genuine. *Undeniably*, which is beyond confusing to reconcile with our present awkward circumstances. Though how much of that awkwardness is all in my own head? Declan must've fallen asleep on the latest drive, too, because there's the indent of a seat belt line across his cheek.

"Good morning," he croaks, his vocal cords still half-asleep.

"Not quite," I say. "Still a whole night ahead. If you can get a hotel room."

He grins, running a hand down his face as he yawns. "I guess we'll find out soon enough, won't we?"

I reach into the back seat and grab my bag for the night, tossing Amelia's hers, as well, before realizing that might be a mistake because her laptop is inside. She catches it no problem, but with urgency, as if her life depends on it.

"If there aren't any rooms, I'm always down to crash on a couch," Grady says.

"I don't know where you'll find a couch, because it won't be ours," Amelia says in a voice that might only be teasing, but it's still very unclear.

Grady hits the lock button, and the SUV beeps. Amelia does the same, twice, to be extra sure it's locked. "I've slept on the floor before," Grady says. "Wouldn't be the first time, won't be the last."

"I hope the back seat of your car is comfy," she says.

"For any particular reason?" Grady teases her back.

This is definitely veering toward flirting. I grab Amelia's arm, and we walk ahead toward the entry.

"Are you into Grady?" I whisper, glancing over my shoulder to make sure the guys aren't close enough behind us to overhear.

"We aren't compatible in the slightest." Amelia says this as if it's obvious.

Through the automatic doors is a narrow lobby, with the check-in situated at the entrance. Ahead there's a sign with arrows to the right for the breakfast area and stairs, and to the left for the pool and elevators.

"But he's trying to flirt with you?" I ask my sister as I lead her over to the counter.

"And sometimes, if I'm feeling game, I'll flirt back. It can just be an extra level of fun friendliness if you're not leading someone on, and trust me, I'm not."

"If you say so."

Amelia greets the worker to check us in. I let her be the big sister who has to deal with the logistics. She approaches it with confidence, our reservation number already pulled up on her phone to confirm our booking without much hassle. I spin on my heels to see the guys as they walk through the glass doors.

"In a rush?" Declan asks.

I shake my head. "Did you see those windmills?" I change the subject. "I was thinking, for the road trip game, maybe this is a stretch, but what if there's aliens? Like, you play as an alien, trying to gain experience points and blend in with humanity, so that's where the pitfalls come in."

Declan is immediately game with this plan. "And something silly, like how filling up a gas tank is a thrilling prospect rather than a chore."

"So we're actually throwing together a team submission?"

"We could work on it tonight."

There's not really a rush since we'll have a couple days when we get back home before the submission deadline, and I could use some space from Declan tonight, actually. "I think Amelia and I might want to check out the pool later."

"Oh, okay. Yeah, no hurry. No reason to pass up a pool."

The clerk slides the key cards over the counter and then we go stand off to the side, waiting for the guys since there's just the one employee working this area right now.

Grady and Declan fall into easy conversation with the guy behind the desk, and while there's a prolonged moment of typing on the computer, Declan turns and gives us a thumbs-up shortly after.

"Looks like they got a room," I tell Amelia, both relieved they won't be sharing a sleeping space with us and mildly irritated that it all went so smoothly, even though I'm glad Declan got the favorable outcome rather than having to scramble to figure something else out. It's just somewhat annoying at the same time. "We're all good. We can head upstairs."

Amelia wiggles in place. "Good, I need to pee."

We hurry down the hall with patterned carpeting and generic paintings on the walls, past large windows that look into the empty swimming pool, and find the elevators in the far corner near the emergency exit.

On our way up to the fourth floor, I ask, "You have more than one swimsuit, right? That we put in the garbage bags."

"Yeah, I have a couple." My sister answers as if this is a general question and not one with another suggestion hidden behind it. She must be too focused on rushing to the bathroom, dancing in place.

As the elevator doors open, I step back and let her bolt out first, but she stops at the divide, waiting for me to read the sign and direct us the correct way down the hall. "To the right," I call out, and without missing another step, she races down the hall. I struggle to keep up. "Why do you have multiple swimsuits?"

She walks tight against the wall, pausing briefly to read one room plaque more closely and deducing that ours is two doors down. "From that one-credit swim class."

"When did you take a swim class?"

She tilts her head back in an *I already told you this* sort of way as she taps the room key against the door reader. It flashes red. "This is our room, right?" she asks.

I reach forward and take the key, trying it again with a little more patience, and it registers as green, the mechanism unlocking and granting us entrance. Amelia pushes past me, drops her things on the desk, and makes it to the bathroom. Leaving the door slightly ajar, she calls out from the toilet, “Why do you need a swimsuit? You want to go swimming?”

It seems like a better idea than sitting around this hotel room stuck in my thoughts. I’d rather float around, weightless and unbothered—if that’s even a state that would be possible for me to achieve tonight.

“The pool was empty,” I shout to her, also setting my stuff down and turning the key card over in my hands. Without waiting for another response, I add, “I’ll go back to the car and find us the swimsuits.”

The reverse course feels longer than our arrival, like the hallway has elongated now that I’m making this trek on my own, and the parking lot seems creepier. Declan and Grady weren’t still in the lobby, so they must be up in a room already. It’s probably not the same floor as ours or I would’ve passed them, but I really have no idea.

I’m sure we’ll touch base at some point tonight, to make plans for tomorrow, at least, so although I’m conflicted, I get ahead of the evening and send Declan a text from the parking lot.

Iris: Hey, yeah, so me and my sister are going to swim in a bit

It’s more of an update than an invitation.

Hopefully, Declan doesn’t have a swimsuit and decides to sit this out, but if not, I can’t wear my hearing aids in the water, so it's not like we'll have to spend much time talking. I could splash around on the opposite end of a rather large indoor pool from him and not have to say much of anything until tomorrow.

There's still nine hours on the road back to Omaha.

•••••

"We haven't matched like this in over a decade," I say as Amelia and I stare at ourselves in the mirror. I found two athletic racer-back one-piece suits, her swimming class attire, with the exact same blue body and orange-outlined straps. "Why do you have two of the same exact swimsuit?"

"It was the one on sale because apparently no one wanted this color." She slides on a pair of shorts. "I got two so that I wouldn't have to wash them as often."

There's no text response from Declan, and I decide to leave my phone in the room, along with my hearing aids; without them in, the world falls into a hushed hum. Without the amplified volume, everything around me fades away, settling into the background like I'm acting in my own movie and the only sounds that matter are the ones I seek out.

The rest is just noise.

It lends a childhood-vacation quality to this night that clashes with how grown-up it feels to be on our own. I'm in a hotel with my sister, in dorky matching swimsuits, but without our parents or any supervision. We're the adults here? That doesn't seem right. The strong chlorine scent takes me back to wanting to cannonball into the deep end, my dad frowning in the distance, and my mom yelling something about not running that I can't quite hear and therefore ignore.

We drop our stuff on an empty table, and Amelia slides into the deep end from the ledge while I walk slowly down the shallow steps. The water isn't cold, but it's not warm, either, and takes adjusting to, but after being scrunched up in the car all day, it feels amazing to submerge and spread my limbs about. I wade forward until the water rises to my chin and I have to stand on my toes to keep above the surface.

Once or twice, there's someone walking past the window in the hallway, but neither Declan nor Grady has shown up. I settle in, feeling like there's a good chance they won't want to join us in the pool, so it can just be my sister and me.

Like this whole trip was supposed to be.

Amelia swims a few laps across the narrow side of the deep end without much effort. She then drifts over in my direction, floating on her back nearby, keeping her voice loud and accessible. "Should I do?" she calls out, but I've missed what she's asking about.

"What?" I ask.

She drops her legs and stands upright beside me. "A triathlon."

"A triathlon?" I'm almost positive I hadn't heard correctly. "Don't you have to, you know, run?"

She scrunches her face. "That part wouldn't be fun. But my friends have been talking about training for one."

"Your swimming-class friends?"

She nods but seems to change her mind as quickly as she made it up. "Though I probably won't have regular access to a pool or bike this summer during the abroad program since we'll be traveling so much. I should see how they do with the race this fall and then decide if I want to join them next year."

"If they hate it, then you never have to do it," I agree.

She laughs. "They won't hate it."

"And you think the running part will be fine enough?"

"It's not like they're going to load up the course with obstacles. I doubt I'd trip," she says, unbothered, before pointing toward the door I hadn't heard or seen open. "I think I can guess who's here."

Declan steps inside the pool area wearing athletic shorts. He says something to us as he drops off his stuff on the same table, sliding off his T-shirt and adding it to the pile.

"Lee, what did Declan say?"

Amelia ignores my question and gives me a pointed look instead. "Just so you know, I'm leaving if Grady shows up."

"I don't understand your friendship with him," I say. "Do you like him or hate him?"

She tilts her head back, considering her words, but there's a trace of a smile creeping onto her face. "No, he's nice and everything, but I can only listen to someone name-drop members of Congress for so long before it becomes too much."

"Okay, but what did Declan just say? I couldn't hear him." I still need her to repeat whatever he said when he arrived.

She dips beneath the water, popping up a few feet away from me, too far for me to catch what she says, so I have to paddle after her.

More childhood flashbacks, honestly—chasing after my sister just to stay in the know. "What?" I insist.

"That Grady's upstairs on a call." She hops around on her toes. "I'll probably swim a few more laps, then head back upstairs so I can shower first."

"You assume you get to shower first?" I tease, crossing my arms.

Also feeling childish, she sticks out her tongue, splashes water in my face, and swims away. I try to follow, but she's actually learned a thing or two in that class, because I can't catch up to her.

Now shirtless, Declan steps toward the pool but doesn't get in. I tiptoe over to the edge in strides, like bouncing across the moon, very similar to the void of space because I can't hear what he's saying. Why isn't he getting in the water? But it's made clear when he points over his shoulder to the hot tub.

"Oh, nice," I say, nodding.

He continues talking as he walks over and hits the button and the bubbles roar to life. He waves again for me to join as he slinks into the water. Maybe I sort of already agreed to when I nodded?

I dip beneath the water, screaming internally.

This is not how I wanted the night to go. But of course I'm going to join him in the freaking hot tub.

We're friends, aren't we? It's normal for friends to hang out together. You know what, I wanted to go sit in the hot tub anyway, so this is fine.

I self-consciously climb up the pool stairs, holding my arms tight across my chest, shivering as I hurry over to the hot tub, plunking down into the warm water.

Cold to hot.

Though fully anticipated, it still sends a shock through my system.

I'm across from Declan, and he says something, but as I sit on this bench, it's still incredibly difficult to hear him with the roar of bubbles at my shoulders. There's too much competition noise, and I've never been the best at lipreading. But also, with Declan, I'm maybe a little distracted.

I just smile and nod, uncharacteristically quiet.

The way he stretches out his neck, I can tell Declan is speaking up a little louder, but I return a vacant smile. Another nod.

What am I doing here?

If he hadn't gathered already, Declan deduces what's going on and slides around the circular bench until he's next to me, close enough that I can pick up on the low register of his voice, just crossing the threshold of what I can catch, and also stare at those lips of his. With a grin, he asks, "You haven't heard a single word I've been saying, have you?"

I smile—for real this time, recognition alight in my eyes—and shake my head.

Which still leaves him guessing. "You can hear me now, though?"

I grin, teeth showing, as I nod, not quite ready to talk since I know my voice will come across louder and unregulated because I can't hear myself, either.

This is something I'm usually not self-conscious about.

Until now.

"No swimsuit?" I ask, but I apparently overcorrected and didn't add enough volume.

He just laughs and slides another inch closer until we're less than an arm's reach away to say, "You're whispering, Iris."

"Right," I say, too loudly, but he doesn't seem bothered. "Just wearing shorts?"

"It was either that or follow your lead and steal from my brother's wardrobe." He shakes his head. "But he didn't have a suit for me to borrow. Well, not of the swimming variety. He's got professional work attire for days."

"Better than nothing," I say, and immediately regret saying the word *nothing* when we're already less dressed than usual. I can't stop the blush spreading across my cheeks.

"Lucky that we got the hot tub without a bunch of kids hanging out in here," he says.

"I think the last time I was in a hot tub was when I was one of those kids hanging out in here." I'm definitely shouting over these bubbles. This is so cringe. "But our parents would make me and Amelia get out if they saw an adult looking angrily in our direction."

I glance over my shoulder to check on Amelia in the pool and catch a glimpse of her leaving out the doorway without saying goodbye, her hair dripping a trail of water in her wake.

"Oh, she left," I say to myself.

Though Declan probably hears. He shrugs.

I don't know what I expected when I decided to go to the pool. Maybe I had some innocent picture of the four of us playing a game—someone finding a Nerf football and breaking into teams, throwing it across the length of the water. Or going back and forth taking turns jumping into the deep end. And maybe, on some other night, we still would've gotten up to more silly antics.

But right now it's just Declan and me in this hot tub.

Chapter Twelve

The atmosphere is markedly different now that it's just Declan and me. This is a big open room, and the large window to the hotel hallway is right there, but despite the occasional passersby, somehow it feels like we're completely alone together with nothing else in sight. Sort of like when we were chatting together on the common room couch, or sitting across the table during a Rivalry match, there's something about spending time with him that can make the rest of the environment fade away.

And there's this new familiarity, I swear.

Take us away from our usual spot, to a place where we don't really know anyone else, and suddenly, after the initial shock of stumbling upon each other on a college campus, it's like we were always this close, like it's only natural for us to share more, to talk about things we never would've talked about on an ordinary day. Somewhat similar to being on vacation and ending up stuck in an elevator with people who are also from Nebraska. The particulars of them living in a different city don't matter because, for a few minutes, it's the most interesting thing in the world to have run into strangers a long way from home and find everyone has something in common.

Everything is scrambled in my mind. I have to trust that I'll be able to hold my tongue and stop myself from blurting out something too revealing, but that's a hard sensation to fight, because one look in his eyes and I feel like I could tell him anything.

Does Declan feel the change too?

But he's relieved I don't have a crush on him, right? That we're friends. There's no reason for me to be entertaining this thought still.

Yet the door doesn't feel fully closed.

I fidget with my fingers beneath the bubbling water. I should call it a night, drag myself out of this hot tub, back into the cold air, wrap myself in a scratchy towel, and chase my sister back to the hotel room, where I'll stand dripping chlorine on the laminate flooring while she takes her sweet time to yield the shower. Then we can find something to put on the TV that doesn't matter because we'll really spend the evening scrolling through our phones before finally falling asleep to get enough rest for another entire day on the road tomorrow.

That sounds nice and relaxing and the total opposite of the racing emotions I'm feeling right now.

I glance up from the water, almost shocked to discover I'm actually still sitting here next to Declan, and he gives a small smile that makes it impossible for me to leave. It'd be incredible to know what he's thinking right now or if he can sense that I'm acting different around him.

He reaches a hand across his chest to scratch his shoulder. "One more long day on the road until we're back home."

I pull my knees up and rest my feet along the edge of the bench seat, sitting against the wall and tilting my chin as I ask, "Where would you have stayed tonight? If not at the hotel?"

Declan narrows his eyes and hunches forward as if sharing a secret. "We've got a tent in the trunk."

"So anywhere, then?"

"I bookmarked a few campgrounds that we pass."

I can't help but continue to tease him. "Don't you need reservations for those too?"

"Sometimes. Not always. If it's peak season, or a really busy spot, but I saw on the map there were always a few lodges near those places too."

"I guess you did have some general idea."

"Of course." He smiles. "But this is fine too."

"It's fine," I agree. "I got to say, though, there's no harm adding some certainty to life. To know there's a place waiting for you."

I look away, skimming my hand along the surface of the water, gathering the remnants of the bubbles in front of me as the timer runs out. This is a great sign to leave, to say good night and go to sleep, but Declan briefly hops out of the water to turn it back on. I lean back against the wall and sigh.

He doesn't return next to me, however. He stays in the middle, crouched beneath the water, waving his arms around to keep upright as he sways on his heels, avoiding looking up at me.

Then he says something I only partly hear. I tilt my head, and Declan repeats, "Strange to think we'll be back in this state for college soon."

"Strange," I echo, pretending the thought hadn't crossed my mind the second we drove across the Ohio-Indiana border, knowing that the next time I'm here, I'll be approaching from the opposite direction, except with a car full of all my things and my own campus ahead of me.

He steps closer, with most of his body still beneath the surface, approaching me at eye level. "There is actually something I've been thinking about saying to you."

My heart races. "Yeah?"

"And I already know how you're going to respond, so this is just a thought I need to get out of my head, and I don't really want to, because it'll probably make things weird, but it's also, like, maybe I should tell you." He pauses, staring off at the wall, refusing to look at me. "You know what? Forget I said anything."

I cross my arms tight, trying to steady myself from how nervous this is making me. "You used a lot of words but haven't actually said much of anything yet, and now you kind of have to . . ."

"I don't know."

"Okay, just tell me, generally, what it's about?"

Declan shakes his head. "That would basically be telling you."

"Then tell me." I shrug. "Because otherwise you're really letting my imagination run wild here."

"I don't think I can. Because what if it's not a good time and what if . . ." He trails off.

My eyebrows scrunch down, and I give him a stern gaze. "Then why did you say you had to tell me something? I feel like we keep getting stuck in standoffs."

He lets out a nervous chuckle. "Checkmate."

"Nope," I say, shaking my head and bringing back levity to my tone. "You're going to tell me, and it'll be fine, I promise."

"You promise?"

"Yeah, Declan." I cross my arms and lean back. "Go ahead."

He takes a deep breath and relents. "Earlier, when I asked you about that text—I said it's awkward," Declan says, eyes wide and vulnerable, holding up a hand since he senses my need to interrupt, and I bite my lip, impatiently waiting to counter whatever he might have to add about the circumstances, when he says, "but it's awkward because I realized that *I* might have a crush on *you*."

"Oh." My head tilts and lips part.

His blue eyes stare into mine. "Yeah."

"Oh?" I repeat.

"Yeah?" he asks this time.

I'm not even trying to play coy; I'm baffled. "Since when?"

Declan winces, squeezing one eye shut, before raising his eyebrows almost hopefully. "I'm not sure. I think it sort of crept up on me."

He looks so cute I can't stand it. My own sentiments come roaring back with a vengeance, stronger than ever. I scramble to reconsider all our previous interactions, but the only thing I can think of right now is him here, in front of me, waiting for me to respond.

Declan notices my hesitation. "Or I'm kidding because we said we're friends and that's one of many reasons why I didn't want to say anything right now." He floats a few inches back. "The chlorine must be going to my head." When he doesn't think he's got a winning hand, he reaches for a joke to suggest he's indifferent to the outcome. He must find one more moment of bravery, however. "But I kind of thought maybe you were also starting to like me too."

I smile wide, unable to play it cool. "Maybe I am?"

He leans back. "Like, I assumed your sister's text was a joke. But later my brother was asking what I thought about you because I kept mentioning that we're going to the same college, and I just really wasn't sure what *you* were thinking, and that would kind of impact what *I* was thinking, right? We've been spending more time together, and it's sort of getting confusing."

I reach my hand through the water and grab onto his arm. I can't find the words, but my body leads the way. I pull him closer, lessening the distance between us to whisper this revelation. "I thought I was being *so* obvious."

Declan takes a deep breath, relief spreading across his face. "I would not say *obvious*."

"If you say so." I hold on tight.

Declan stares at me. "Iris, nothing about you is obvious."

I look at the water, unable to meet his gaze as I say, "You're one to talk. You should have told me."

"I just did."

"You did." I smile. "You *like* me."

He inches closer. "And you like me too?"

"I think we've established that," I tease.

Declan reaches out to tuck a strand of hair behind my ear in a way that feels surprisingly confident, contrary to the affirmation he asks for again. "Want to spell it out for me?"

"I like you too." There's barely any space left between us and a sort of moment of inevitability as I sense our lips are close enough to almost touch. "Now what?" I whisper, adding with a slight giggle, "I think we're about to kiss."

Our mouths find contact, yet my thoughts are struggling to compute.

It's . . . well, it's something.

Declan's lips are pressed against mine, firm in a way that feels hesitant, unsure, and awkward. Before I can contemplate how my own lips are contributing to this, he's already withdrawn from me, a confused smile dawning on his face.

"What?" I ask, second-guessing everything, left feeling like *really, that's it?* Did he think that was a good kiss? Or *was it* a good kiss and I've forgotten how kissing works? Maybe we're just nervous.

"I did not think that was something you and I would ever do." He looks equally mystified by the circumstances.

I'm relieved to address this, hoping that might help unpack

how this kiss didn't feel cinematic in the slightest, with no immediate fireworks or butterflies in my stomach. Even right now I feel like I'm already debriefing with friends rather than sitting with a crush in a hot tub gearing up to kiss again. "Kind of weird, isn't it?"

Declan laughs, and glances over his shoulder to the hallway window. "I kept wanting to make sure there wasn't someone watching us or something."

"That would *really* make it weird."

We stare at each other in a way that still feels comfortable, despite whatever this speed bump is.

"It's not that late yet," Declan says, glancing over to the clock on the opposite wall.

I guess we're not gonna try more kissing anytime soon? I don't want to appear too disappointed, so I stand to climb the stairs. "We could borrow Amelia's laptop and work on the road trip game?" Staying here at the pool doesn't feel like the right move.

"Sure."

Declan follows me out of the water, and we trail over to the towel rack, drying off before we slide our other clothes back on. I slip into my sneakers, the socks still balled up at the toes, folding down the worn heels, a temporary measure to get my wet feet back upstairs to the hotel room. I give my hair an extra scrunch or two until it stops dripping, then toss the towel into the nearby bin and walk back toward our stuff.

"But first, could we try this again?" Declan steps quickly toward me, intercepting my path and wrapping his arms around my waist. I instinctively hook my own behind his neck, drawing our faces close together, our lips finding each other once more with soft, warm, wonderfully inviting certainty.

Slow, at first, with confidence multiplying by the second . . .

Until this is the only thing that makes sense, with the biggest question being why hadn't we thought to try this sooner? Followed by a more cosmic thought: If we hadn't run into each other this week, what are the chances that we would have ever found our way to a kiss like this one?

Declan reaches a hand up to my hair, and I sigh against his lips, delighted it won't take us long to get accustomed to this new game together.

Chapter Thirteen

Declan and I walk through the hallway, bumps rising on my arms that are only marginally related to how cold it feels out of the hot tub. The elevator takes a minute to arrive, then the doors open slowly. I hold up four fingers, and he presses buttons for both of our floors. We stand side by side, staring forward until we arrive on the third. I nudge my arm against his shoulder in a brief farewell.

"See you in a few?" Declan asks, waiting for my nod before he steps out of the elevator.

As the silver doors close, I'm confronted by a hazy reflection of my own cheesy grin.

I don't have the key, so I knock on the hotel room door twice before calling my sister. She takes her time letting me in, stifling a big yawn and wearing an oversized green Audubon College T-shirt.

"Were you asleep already?" I ask.

"No," she admits, plopping back into bed to continue scrolling. She says something else, so I have to walk closer to catch her repetition since I still don't have my hearing aids in. "How was the pool?"

"You could've said goodbye." I shake my head. "But can I borrow your laptop?"

She doesn't look up from her phone. "What? Why?"

"Declan and I are going to work on the road trip game we've been brainstorming."

"Isn't it late?" Amelia yawns again.

"It's not even eleven yet. I see why you drink so much caffeine."

She closes her eyes briefly. "This hotel better have decent coffee tomorrow morning."

"I'm guessing you don't want to come hang out?" I almost add *again* to guilt her into it, but given that she's horizontal right now, the odds of her leaving this room are slim. Plus, doesn't part of me sort of hope it could just be me and Declan tonight?

"Nah, I've spent enough time with Grady today." Oh, right, Grady will be in Declan's room. She raises an arm and points across the room to where her backpack is on the corner chair. "But my laptop's over there."

"Thank you."

I dig out my pajamas—sweatpants and a similar oversized tee—and go shower, untangling the knots and rinsing all the pool water from my hair and then standing there in the steam wondering if my sister has even the slightest suspicion that I've kissed Declan.

As I dry out my ears and put my hearing aids back in, I ask Amelia, "Are you sure you want to stay here?"

"Don't forget to take the key with you," she says, pointing again to her backpack, then to the dresser where the two room cards are.

•••••

I text Declan that I'm on my way to the third floor, and he meets me by the elevator. He's wearing athletic shorts and a *Jurassic Park* shirt and holding a few soda bottles from the vending machine. "I hope you're hungry, because Grady can never resist playing host."

"Oh, really?" I ask, reaching for one of the drinks.

Declan and I approach the identical room, almost directly below where Amelia is upstairs, where Grady has an assortment of chips, crackers, and cookies on the wooden hotel table. He's sitting in the rolling chair, ankle crossed over his knee, halfway through a pack of Doritos.

"You kids left the pool to do homework?" Grady smirks, holding up his cheesy fingers pressed together, hand outstretched like he's in the middle of a stump speech.

"Hey, there's a deadline," Declan says. "We don't have much time to throw this together."

Now, standing shoulder to shoulder with Declan, I once again wonder if it's obvious that we've kissed. Declan takes a seat atop the comforter, and with Grady already in the chair, my only seating options are the other bed or next to Declan.

Or the floor, but that's nasty.

I take my time getting Amelia's laptop out of her backpack and plugging it into the wall before sitting on the edge of the bed, opposite Declan. Grady tosses me some Oreos before opening his own laptop to do some other work of his own while Declan and I lean together to share a screen.

It only takes an hour or so to consolidate our individual notes and get an initial picture of how this board will come together.

"Like a country map," Declan suggests, but not fully sold on the idea himself. "That seems a little too Ticket to Ride, you know?"

"Yeah, but I wouldn't want it to be too Monopoly or Life, either." I frown at the document. Declan leans back on his elbows, against my legs. I take a slow breath. "I guess it depends on the outcomes. Are the players all going on the exact same trip, or are there variations?"

"It would be nice to have different paths. That's something we could manage with cards, though," he suggests.

"And dice," I tease.

"I think Ticket to Ride has a dice expansion, though . . ." He runs the back of his hand against his scrunched-up forehead, trying to think. "I mean, we're not going to be reinventing the wheel here."

"True." If we're having trouble differentiating enough anyway, maybe we need to pull even more familiar inspiration. An idea strikes then, and I'm giddy. "What if we combine it with something like Battleship? Like, what if there's aliens on the ground on the road but navigators that are up in the sky, and it's more of a cooperative game, but one that's high risk because you don't know if you're going to be helpful or, like, accidentally smite your teammate somehow?"

Declan matches my energy immediately, sitting back up and pointing to the screen. "Then we can do maps, but separate ones that other players can't see rather than a shared one on the table."

"Exactly."

We lock eyes, and I'm so entranced by how well we're working together that I almost forget where we are—until Grady bursts out laughing at something on his computer. Declan and I smile, looking away, but his fingers graze across my hand on the keyboard.

Another two hours pass in a matter of minutes, and we've planned out this entire board game, complete with a quick mock-up we can print and assemble after more fine-tuning back home. But it's definitely time to get some sleep because of the very real road we have to traverse tomorrow. Well, *today*, since it's nearly two in the morning, not to get annoying-kid-at-the-sleepover about this.

"All that's left is to figure out a name," I say.

"That's tricky." Declan hides a yawn in his shoulder, mirroring the roaring dinosaur on his tee. "I'm not great with coming up with names."

"Yeah, *Numbers*, I know that." I save the files and reluctantly slip off the bed to put the laptop back in the backpack. "I'm sure we'll think of something on the way."

"And see if we can convince Amelia and Grady to make a stop or two," he agrees. We researched and found some weird little roadside attractions as inspiration to incorporate into the game, a few of which might be reasonable to see in person on our final driving stretch back to Omaha.

Grady gets up to go to the bathroom and brush his teeth as I head over to the door and step into my shoes.

"Need me to walk you back to your room?" Declan asks, standing as well.

"Not really . . ." Until it dawns on me half a second later. "Oh, sure."

"To the elevator, at least," Declan says, grabbing his hotel key card and following me out the door.

Grady shouts something after us, which I can only guess must've been "Smooth!" So it seems he has sensed the dynamic shift.

Declan and I make our way down the hall, and it's like I forget how to be around him. We walk several feet apart, not looking at each other or saying anything, and then out of nervousness, I hit the call button right away. I probably could've waited a minute or two to do that, but when I spin back around to face him, we fall into each other's arms again, ignoring the elevator doors opening and closing behind us.

•••••

At the breakfast area the next morning, there are a few business travelers filling up bowls and plates with pastries and cereal before taking seats at the tables scattered around the lobby dining area. There's a family with young toddlers, but no one else our age around, at least until Declan and Grady walk into the lobby, too, with their bags in tow, ready to leave after we eat.

Amelia passes me a plate and grabs one for herself. "What looks good?" she asks, leaning over a tray of muffins to observe more closely.

"Those are chocolate chip. And maybe bran. I can't tell what the other ones are," I narrate, taking a step closer to her. "A couple different cereal options. Oatmeal. Pancake machine."

My sister perks up at the challenge of making her own one-minute fresh breakfast. "Where's the pancakes?"

"Straight ahead on the counter." I stick a bowl underneath the cinnamon cereal, which spills down in a larger quantity than I'll be able to stomach this morning, as I squint toward the pancake-making device. "I think you put the plate underneath on the right, then press the button on the left."

"Easy enough," Amelia says. "Want one?"

"Nah."

Back at the table, we all settle in to eat and plan the day. Grady has three bananas stacked next to his plate, which I assume are to be brought with for later, but it'll be amusing if he tries to eat them all right now. That's got to be too much potassium.

I slide my phone across to Amelia, with one of the roadside attractions pulled up on the map.

Yet the only thing my sister seems to notice is how much time it adds to our journey. "You really want to delay getting home by at least forty-five minutes?" She pinches the screen to zoom in and read what I've added to the route. "Just to see some *mustard*?"

I reach forward to grab back my phone. "It's the world's largest bottle of mustard, thank you very much." With a chuckle, I add, "The aliens find it fascinating."

"You're not making any sense." Amelia rolls her eyes and takes a slow sip of her coffee, and I know she won't be receptive right now to further explanations about the board game development.

"It won't take that long," I reassure her. "No more than a twenty-minute detour at most."

She takes another long sip. "Each way. That's an hour."

"You're terrible at math."

"I'm tired, and I want to get home. It was an exhausting week of finals, and this is terrible coffee."

Grady peels open his first banana. "I'm more of a *cat*sup guy myself," he jokes.

Amelia rolls her eyes. "Even when spelled the other way, it's still pronounced *ketchup*."

"Is she always this grumpy in the mornings?" Grady asks me, but the only answer is Amelia's knife loudly scraping her plate as she cuts into the pancake again.

Declan blinks a few times in the ensuing silence, jaw tightening as he tries to keep the peace. "If it's too out of the way, we don't have to make the stop."

"No, really," I insist, remembering how much fun we had laughing about this last night, and having already envisioned us stopping there for a picture, I'm not letting go of it that easily. "It's really not a problem. What's the point of a road trip if we don't make a few stops along the way?"

"This isn't a road trip, though," Amelia says. "We're driving the car home from school."

"On the road," I say. "Sounds like a trip."

"As long as it really doesn't add too much time," Grady says, turning to his brother. "Mom and Dad are waiting for us to get back."

"All the more reason I'm happy to take my time," Declan mutters, eyes narrowed and forehead wrinkled. Grady gives him a skeptical look but doesn't press.

Amelia likes to get in the final word. "It's fine. One stop. That mustard better be worth it."

I smile wide, already envisioning her frustration when we drive out of the way only for it to almost certainly not meet her expectations of what's *worth it*. "That's a lot of pressure on a roadside attraction."

Chapter Fourteen

Despite grabbing a second to-go cup of coffee, Amelia's been in a grouchy mood all morning. It's like she used up all her pleasantries yesterday and now can't be bothered. She's slumped in the passenger seat, too irritated to even want to scroll through her phone, arm outstretched to advance through every song in my playlist after only thirty seconds.

"A second verse wouldn't kill you," I say, trying to keep my tone light, knowing this could be interpreted as a joke or a fight-starter, and honestly, I'm fine with either.

She skips ahead faster, as soon as the song titles display on the screen. "I don't want to listen to anything."

"We could sit in silence."

"That's somehow worse." But she gives up and lets the Olivia Rodrigo song we've landed on play out, letting out a groan as she turns to stare out the window. "I just want to be home already."

"Yeah, you've mentioned." I sigh and change lanes, glancing at the ETA on the GPS, which shows another eight hours and fifty-two minutes. The time change going back into Central will give us an hour back, but that will basically even out with having to get food and gas and brief sightseeing. "We'll get there when we get there" slips out of my mouth before I can process that's what Mom would always say whenever we complained on a road trip.

Amelia holds her phone up close to her face, reading through a zoomed-in message screen. "I know, but I want to get back tonight to see my friends."

"That has to be *tonight*?"

"Brielle's family is leaving for vacation tomorrow, and she doesn't get back until after I'm already in Europe, so, yeah, it kind of has to be tonight. I told them that I would be able to catch them after dinner."

The check engine light flickers on the dash, and all I can do is sigh. "If we make it home."

"What?" Amelia says.

Has it been on all morning and I'm only noticing it now? I really don't want to deal with this. The car is running fine. Sometimes in the winter when it's cold, random lights on the dash turn on and off and there's never any problem.

"What do we do about this?" I ask.

"About what?" At least I have Amelia's full attention now. She's dropped her phone into her lap.

I'd sort of forgotten that I hadn't voiced the situation out loud. "The freaking check engine light is on."

She groans. "Really? Do you know what's wrong?"

"Oh, yeah, it's obvious."

"What?"

I roll my eyes, annoyed she's not picking up on my sarcasm. "Lee, the light went from off to on, and that's literally all I know."

My sister ignores my snark and jumps into action mode. "What color is it?"

I glance in the rearview mirror first, at a car speeding up behind us, before checking the dash again. "Orange—does that make a difference?"

"Should I call Dad?"

"What's he going to do about it?" I ask, glancing down to the dash once more, hoping it's gone away already.

We're on a small highway, with only one lane going in each direction, a thick division of trees between, and a truly tragic amount of roadkill. The white SUV is directly ahead, and I've probably wondered about Declan glancing back at me more often than he actually has.

Amelia shakes her head. "I think we should ask Dad if—"

"Oh!" I shout, hit with genuine relief. The light has turned off. "It's gone."

"Gone?" she asks.

"Yep."

"Are you sure?"

"Lee . . . the light went from on to off." I repeat the words but inverse the order, like a hacky stand-up bit. "I don't know what to tell you. The light is no more."

She takes a deep breath. "Should I call Mom and let her know, though?"

"I think we're all good. We can call them if this happens again." I relax into the driver's seat and turn up the volume on Sabrina Carpenter.

•••••

We stop at a gas station that's close to where we need to veer off our established path in order to get to the world's largest bottle of mustard. While I fill the tank, Amelia needs to run inside to pee, and Grady offers to tag along to help her find the bathroom. He emerges a few minutes later, looking delighted with a new pair of cheap sunglasses, while Amelia returns harrowed by a disgusting toilet.

I glance to the next pump, where Declan's standing next to the SUV, and consider suggesting that we do some car-swapping again today, but Amelia and Grady have already gotten into our respective vehicles, so I don't want to rock the boat before we get to the mustard.

"I'll text you the location," Declan calls over to me as he closes the gas tank and walks back to the driver's side door. "It's not like a street address or anything, just a pin on the map, so I have no idea what area we're showing up to."

"Me either!" Still, I'm giddy.

We're on the highway for another couple of minutes before veering off at a random, isolated exit. We follow the directions onto a narrow, bumpy road, not passing much of anything except a couple of boarded-up old houses. Through the trees, I catch a glimpse of our destination only moments before we arrive and have to quickly swerve to the side of the road, where the pressed-down grass indicates this is the only available parking.

Declan and Grady park behind us, with just enough room for both of our vehicles to be off the road, but there isn't any oncoming traffic anyway.

I get out of the car and walk around to the other side to join my sister as we take a few steps closer to the structure.

Amelia squints up past the tall trees lining the road to look at the faded golden paint of the giant bottle atop the raised black steel platform. She crosses her arms. "This is it?"

The world's largest bottle of mustard is a former water tower, built and designed to resemble the product of the mustard company that used to be in this town, and in the years since, the novelty of this structure has led to it being repaired and anointed a historic attraction.

It's quaint in a way most tourist traps aren't these days. No gift shop hawking merch, for one. Just a random old structure that doesn't even have a good vantage point for a photo.

"The experience points on this one are probably overvalued," Declan jokes, holding out his phone to take a picture of the giant bottle, then he nods for me to pose.

I smile and point up to the base of the tower, knowing we aren't really capturing the full bottle. "Who are we to judge what the aliens find important?"

"Seriously, what's all this about aliens?" Amelia asks, slowly inching her way back to the car, ready to get the show back on the road.

"It's the board game they designed," Grady answers, falling into step with my sister. "To submit for the expo contest."

Amelia gently scuffs the gravel side of the road with her sneaker. "But you were doing the one with the witches?"

"Yeah, I already submitted that," I say. "But there's a team category that we're going to try to get this one in for."

"Okay, well, got the picture you wanted?" she says.

"Actually, one second, I want to get one where we can actually read the label," I say, breaking into a light jog down the road to improve my vantage point. Declan tags along.

"Hurry up, your sister wants to get home!" Grady calls after us.

"She's already well aware," Amelia says, getting back into the car, less than politely waving off Grady as he tries to continue talking and shutting the door behind her, so he goes back to the SUV.

After a few more paces, I slow and turn around, only to notice the trees are now more in the way, even if we can get a slightly better read on the bottle's label.

I take a picture but shake my head. "I'm not sure this is any better," I tell Declan.

He holds his own phone as high as possible without looking at the screen as he takes another shot, then pulls it back to view the image. "Hmm, the higher up, the better the photo. Here, let me try picking you up."

"Really?" I ask, but step toward him, and he bends down to grab my hips and lift me up. I reach my hand high and take the photo, doubting that this was any higher than the image he already took himself, but I don't object to these circumstances. Emboldened and not caring if anyone's looking back at us through the car mirrors, I squeeze my arms around his shoulders and lean to plant a soft kiss on his cheek.

"Any better?" He sets me back on the ground, flushed, still standing close to me.

"Maybe added half an inch," I tease, readjusting my shirt. "Thanks, though."

Declan smiles as we walk back toward the cars. "This should probably be the last stop. The older sibs seem cranky."

"They must've stayed up past their bedtimes. I didn't realize how long we'd be working on the game last night."

"Good thing we'll have time to finish it when we get back home too."

With my elbow, I playfully nudge his arm. "Perhaps even spending time together not talking about or playing board games?"

"I think that can be arranged," Declan says with a wink.

Chapter Fifteen

The GPS doesn't want us to turn back around the way we entered, so we have to take another winding road that supposedly will somehow bring us to the highway, but our old car is struggling on this uneven pavement.

Amelia is obsessively watching the minutes tick up on our arrival time, as if an extra half hour or so is really going to make that much of a difference in the plans with her friends later. They can just hang out at someone's house late into the evening; there's not really any discernable time crunch here, but my sister won't relax, and it's stressing me out.

I breathe easier once the highway is in sight.

Except when I pull onto the on-ramp and merge us onto the highway, our vehicle's shaking only gets worse.

"Is the check engine light on again?" Amelia asks.

"No." But none of this seems right, and a faint scent of something burning catches my attention.

Smoke billows up from the engine, swirling and obscuring my windshield view.

Amelia reaches forward to slap on the hazard lights. "What are you waiting for? Pull over!"

"On the side of the highway?" I shriek.

"Where else?" She's whipping her head back and forth, trying to look out the side and back windows, making sure our course is clear.

Fortunately already in the right lane, I pull onto the edge strip, over the warning bumps, and skid to a stop, slamming on the brakes, feeling my heart ready to fly out of my chest. "Um, now what?" I say, watching the smoke continue to pour from under the hood.

Amelia is already scrambling for our phones, shoving them into her bag. "We should get out." She opens the passenger door and shouts, "Don't go on that side!"

I climb over the center and join her on the side of the road. The sharp gusts of wind from the high-speed traffic cause my hair to go haywire, getting caught in my eyelashes, which makes the giant looming dragonflies even more terrifying as they circle us among the tall grasses.

Holding my flyaway strands to my head with both hands, I observe our car. The smoke seems to be dissipating, and the whole situation looks much less serious than when we were observing it from inside the windshield, but I'm not exactly eager to get back in.

Amelia says something I can't hear over the traffic.

"What?" I shout to her.

"Shit," she repeats. Lee adds a couple other curses under her breath, standing there with her hands on her hips in a very take-charge manner, analyzing the scene and deciding what she'll do next.

Meanwhile, my eyes are watering. My hair must've scratched the cornea or something, I tell myself, but my heavy gasping and pounding heart suggest other factors at play. We're somewhere in Iowa along the side of the highway and my brain is setting off all sorts of warning bells and whistles, making it difficult for me to calm down.

Squinting down the horizon, I notice that the SUV has pulled over as well and is waiting alongside the road. Amelia hands me my phone, which is ringing, already with a couple other missed calls from Declan.

I answer, and he launches into a question before I can even say hello. "Are you all right?" Declan says.

"Uh, everything's either fine or the car might blow up," I shout over the noise of the highway.

Amelia nudges me farther away from the vehicle. I really don't want to step into more of this itchy grass and sacrifice myself to these huge prehistoric bugs, yet some of these cars are really driving by fast.

It's loud on Declan's end now too. He must've gotten out of the SUV. "We're walking over," he yells.

"Careful!" I shout back, hanging up as soon as I see him and his brother trailing the rocky edge of the pavement next to the greenery. I turn to Amelia, realizing we should probably alert our parents to the situation, "Should we call—"

She's already on her phone and pulls it away from her ear to say, "Mom says to stay here out of the car and wait for a tow. Dad's going to text the number for Triple A for us to call."

Our family's other car broke down once before, when Amelia, Mom, and I were on the way to visit our grandma in the hospital. It is one of the only times I remember seeing my mom cry, the situation compounded by the stress of everything she was going through. My typically level-headed, always-addresses-a-crisis-head-on mother was reduced to a puddle of tears, mumbling *It's one thing, then another* to herself over and over again, her fingers wrapped around the steering wheel as the car stalled out in the middle of a busy road and refused to start back up.

Only nine years old, I stared out the back window, but that was no excuse, because ten-year-old Amelia jumped into action to pick up the slack. She called Dad at work to come get us, gave Mom her water bottle and made her drink to help calm down, and then, for good measure, my sister flipped off all the annoyed drivers who kept giving our car the bird as they struggled to move around the obstruction during rush hour traffic, which made me giggle and lightened the overall mood as we waited.

I want to channel that energy, to be good in a crisis, but I'm hiccupping, still fighting back tears.

"It's all right," Amelia says, pulling away from the phone once more, hearing me sniffle. "Triple A will be here soon."

"You called them already?" Reaching out, I drag my sister's arm to move her away from another circling dragonfly.

"On the call," she mouths, nodding toward my phone and putting the speaker of hers under my chin. "Can you read the card number that Dad just texted?"

Consulting the group chat, I read aloud the number for the AAA representative waiting on the other end, then Amelia puts the phone back to her ear. "Did you get that?" She nods and continues arranging our tow.

"What happened?" Grady calls out. The guys are finally nearby and watching the smoke emit from the car's hood.

"No idea. It started shaking and then all this smoke," I say, gesturing to Amelia as she wraps up the phone call. "We're getting it towed."

"Dang." Declan shakes his head and looks from the car to all the vehicles speeding by on the highway before swatting at what must've been the sound of a bug buzzing by his ear. "Good spot to wait . . ."

"You guys don't have to stay," I insist, feeling like it's somehow my fault that we're all going to be stuck here. "I don't know how long it will all be. You can head on home and—"

Declan gives me an angry look, his brow furrowed in a way I've only seen once before, when he was wrapping up that call in the Roll Again storage closet. "You seriously think I'm going to leave you here on the side of the highway?"

"No, it's just—"

"That's never going to happen." He wraps his arms around me, and I no longer care what our siblings may or may not have picked up on as I lay my head against his chest, listening to his heart beat just as fast as mine is.

"We can all go sit in the SUV," Grady offers.

Amelia hangs up the phone. "I'd rather wait here."

The look on my sister's face right now is downright murderous, but Grady doesn't seem deterred. "Isn't that the whole point of having a support vehicle on this journey? So you don't have to stand on the side of the highway?"

"They said it'll only be about ten minutes," Amelia counters, shaking her head as a bug flies too close to her, causing her to growl and wave her hands around in commanding frustration.

"I guess ten minutes isn't too bad," Grady replies, undaunted. He's doing his best to channel his cheery voice, the one that has a tendency to feel fake, but right now it has an air of reassurance and stability. Like we could all scream and cry and rage yet he'd still be here, with that ridiculous smile on his face, ready to make the best of the situation. He reaches forward to guide the persistent dragonfly away from my sister while handing her his water bottle. "Here. Have something to drink."

I know this mood of Amelia's all too well and half expect her to slap the bottle away, but she accepts it and takes a sip, looking back up at Grady with a warm, grateful smile. I blink from the roadside debris in my eye . . . and from the feeling of déjà vu.

•••••

The big tow truck arrives, pulling off the highway ahead of our car. Even though I know they're coming to our rescue, it's frightening to watch a giant vehicle veer in our direction. The mechanic who hops out is younger than I expected, close to our age, with spiky blue hair and a tailored jumpsuit with a name tag that reads SAM.

They walk around our car, checking it briefly to make sure there's no imminent risk, before heading over to us. "Hey, you all all right?"

"We're okay," Amelia says.

"It's not going to blow up?" I ask, feeling ridiculous for asking while also needing verbal confirmation.

Sam chuckles. "Not typically." Then they hold out a finger, counting the four of us. "Though I've only got room to drive two. I thought you said—"

"Don't worry," Grady reassures, gesturing farther up the highway. "We have another car parked down that way and just walked back to make sure everything was okay."

"Oh, good." Sam nods. "Do you have the keys?"

I'm reluctant to admit this in front of my sister, but, hey, we had to evacuate quickly. "I think I left them in the car. It should still be unlocked."

"Not a problem," Sam says. "Y'all can wait in the truck while I load this all up."

We walk over, and Grady opens the large side door, offering a hand to help me, then Amelia up into the truck. "We'll drive along behind you guys?"

"Sounds good," my sister says, squeezing Grady's palm in appreciation before letting go.

I lock eyes with Declan, who gives a small wave as he and his brother venture back up the highway to wait in their SUV.

His expression is inscrutable, though. I didn't mean to offend him by suggesting they could drive on without us, because it just felt like the obvious, polite thing to offer. Of course I'd prefer if he stays with us. He has to know that, right?

Wrapped around the truck's rearview mirror is a little crochet chain with flowers made from light blue, pink, and white yarn, as well as a small lavender air freshener pouch. There's a cooler of water bottles in the footwell.

Amelia and I are quiet as we wait, and the fear of what's just happened hits me harder in the aftermath. We're the adults here. The ones who had to figure out how to manage a broken-down car on the side of the highway far away from home. And we still don't know how long the repairs will take, or exactly how far we still are from home, but there's at least four more hours left to go.

My sister rose to the occasion. I didn't.

I'm so used to my parents being there to take care of everything. Or, for most of my life, Amelia. But I'm leaving home in a few months, and while I know my family will still be there for me, they won't actually be *there*.

The bench seat squeaks beneath us as I rest my head on my sister's shoulder, grateful she's here with me now.

•••••

At the mechanic, Declan and I wait outside while Amelia and Grady manage the situation in the shop. We excused ourselves after it began to seem too crowded in there, and there's a perfectly good picnic table out here for us to sit at. We're close together on the same side of the table, elbows resting side by side as we check our phones.

"How long do you think it'll take to fix?" I ask when I can't tolerate the quiet anymore.

Declan ponders for a second before he shakes his head. "I know absolutely nothing about cars."

A few minutes later, our siblings exit through the open garage doors rather than the main entrance we originally walked into earlier. Amelia is holding papers, while Grady's hands are clasped together. They're bringing big we've-already-got-it-figured-out energy.

Which is exactly how I know a plan has been made that will only now be relayed to Declan and me, without our input.

"We've got it sorted," Grady announces, resting his palms on the edge of the picnic table, narrowly missing a questionable patch of bird poop.

Amelia hands me the yellow papers, which look like a receipt or something. "The credit card is already on file, and they've got Mom's number for any questions, but this should all be wrapped up in about two hours."

"Oh, nice!" But I look down at the pages, wondering why she handed them to me.

She continues, "Since we're only about four hours out, Mom and Dad said they're fine with you just waiting here until it's ready."

My eyebrows drop down so fast. "Wait, me?"

"Yeah, I'll go ahead and give Lee a ride back," Grady explains, all buddy-buddy with my sister, who now seemingly has no qualms whatsoever about his usage of her nickname.

I stand and confront Amelia. "What? You're just going to leave?"

She gestures toward Declan and then toward a single-story brick building nearby. "You two aren't in a rush. Sam mentioned the roller rink that's right there is a good spot to hang out and wait."

I spin around and discover that Declan's face is contorted and looks even more upset than I feel. He quickly jumps up and follows his brother to the SUV.

"Seriously?" I ask Amelia.

"What?" she asks. "I'll be able to get home to see my friends, and you get to roller-skate with your boyfriend."

I cross my arms so tightly it hurts, but I don't release them. "I told you, no *boyfriend* jokes like that."

"Just playing matchmaker," Amelia adds with a smile, so sure that she's doing something in my best interests.

"I didn't ask you to."

"But it all works out," she insists, genuinely not seeming to see my problem with the situation.

"You could've asked me first, at least. You always just decide what's going to happen and then tell me."

"I don't *always* do that," she says, latching on to what she assumes to be hyperbole. That's the worst part about arguing with my sister—that anything that could be perceived as even the slightest exaggeration somehow negates the entire point. Maybe she doesn't take control of the plans 100 percent of the time, but I wouldn't put that number lower than 90. "Come on, isn't this exactly what you would've come up with here anyway?"

"I don't know, but if—"

"It's a win-win situation here," she interrupts. "Really, what's the alternative?"

I'm not sure, and can't come up with a retort quickly enough, because Declan is returning to the picnic table, carrying his backpack in hand by a single strap, his shoulders slumped, and he doesn't seem enthusiastic about this, either.

Wait, why is Declan upset about this? Does he not want to spend more time with me? Ugh, this is so frustrating.

Grady jogs behind him to catch up, handing over a plastic grocery bag of snacks. "Did you text—"

Declan grits his teeth. "Yeah, I texted Mom. So *you* have to text Dad."

Letting Declan's irritation bounce off him, Grady nods and turns to me. "All good?" he asks, still with that ridiculous smile that right now I'm finding exceptionally patronizing.

Do I really have any choice here? Declan's eyes are wide, deferring to me.

"I mean, it's fine," I say, trying to seem happy enough for Declan to understand I'm glad to spend more time with him but mad enough for my sister to know I'm annoyed she's ditching me again.

"Just saving time," Amelia says in a joking tone, trying to lighten the mood. "I'm kind of jealous that I don't get to roller-skate." I roll my eyes and add a juvenile huff so that she gets the audio effect. "Anyway, the keys are in the shop, and Sam has your number, but you should probably check back in like an hour to see if they finished up early."

"Sure." I lean against the picnic table as Declan sits back down on the bench.

"Are we really roller-skating?" he asks as our siblings wave goodbye and walk across the lot. "I'd rather not."

I wouldn't mind skating, but I won't drag him onto the rink. "Hanging out in air-conditioning seems better than staying here, at least."

"Sure." He stands again.

Grady climbs into the SUV, but Amelia runs back toward the auto shop. "Almost forgot my driving glasses!" She fetches the case from our car, gives another round of goodbyes, then leaves with Grady, abandoning Declan and me to fend for ourselves here in Iowa.

"You know, if they asked us first, we probably would've been cool with them wanting to drive ahead separately," I admit to Declan, reaching out to grab hold of his hand. "But they didn't even bother to consult with us. And then, when I try to tell her why that bothers me, she just brushes it off like she knows best. Like, doesn't what I'm feeling matter at all?"

"Yeah," he says, but his hand feels tense in my grasp, so I intertwine our fingers and spin myself in toward his chest, tilting my chin up with what I hope is a flirty look. He gives a half smile down at me.

"We can make the best of it, though?" I ask.

He doesn't say anything but plants a sweet kiss on my forehead that makes all my concerns melt away.

Chapter Sixteen

Directly inside the building is a small party room on the right, with dark carpet patterned with neon concentric circles and squiggles, and every inch of wall space occupied by arcade games. There are two girls who are laser focused on the claw machine in the corner, clearly attempting to win a very specific stuffed penguin that's in the bottom corner and should be an easy grab, but they stomp their feet as it slips through their metal grasp.

Other than those children and a worker behind the rentals desk, the building is empty on this Thursday afternoon. There are posters on the wall advertising upcoming themed events—including a singles night—so I guess this place stays in business, despite feeling and looking like a relic from the past.

The primary attraction is obviously the rink itself, a large oval of polished wooden floor encased by a wall about four feet tall. There's a disco ball hanging directly in the center, and other colorful flashing lights moving around to shine across the room.

"Should we grab something to eat?" Declan asks, pointing to the counter. "If we're not skating, we should probably still spend money somehow."

I nod toward his backpack, where he stashed away the grocery bag from Grady. "Even though we have all those snacks?"

We take another step toward the menu board. "Maybe nachos?" he suggests.

"Sure."

He pays, and the worker slides a small paper tray of chips across the counter, nodding toward the cheese dispenser next to the napkins, utensils, and straws. Declan chuckles as he drizzles the orange goo atop.

We choose a table, and I climb onto the tall chair, finding myself mesmerized by the light show on the empty rink. It's easy to imagine this place in its heyday, with plenty of skaters rolling around.

"I haven't skated in years." I wave my hand, turning down the nachos as Declan holds the bowl out to me. "Amelia and I used to roller-skate up and down the sidewalk in front of our house."

"That sounds fun. I was more into bikes."

"I didn't like riding my bike because Amelia was so much better at it. She was always first to figure things out, like how to ride a bike without training wheels or how to tie her shoes. And I know that makes sense because she's older, but it always just seemed like she was inherently better at everything than me."

"Well, you know that's obviously not true," Declan says, but he only seems to be half listening.

"Right," I agree. "Though she still seems to think I'm that little kid she needs to take charge of or make arrangements to get out of her hair."

If Amelia were here, we'd probably be skating, though. She wouldn't want us to sit around being boring like this, not when there's something interesting we could be doing instead.

"Maybe we should—" I start, but realize Declan isn't listening at all. He's been lost in his own thoughts, equally annoyed to have been ditched by our siblings, by the look of it, not clueing me into what exactly he's been thinking. His phone buzzes with a text message, which he glances at but doesn't respond to.

"Let's see how Grady enjoys having to spend time later with Mom and Dad all by himself," he mutters.

"You're glad to not be getting home yet?" I clearly understand this is about his frustration with his parents and his brother, but it's also the first glimpse I'm getting that he considers being stuck with me the preferred outcome. "What's wrong?"

Declan averts his eyes to the empty rink, where the song has changed to a more upbeat tempo and the lights are flashing with more dramatic frequency. He gives up on the rest of the nachos and wipes his fingers on a napkin. "I don't want to bore you."

I lean forward, trying to be encouraging. "I've been complaining about my sister; it's your turn."

"But it's boring," he says, yet the words slide out of his mouth, almost desperate to be voiced aloud. "My parents are getting divorced, oh no." He shakes his head, trying to act unbothered, but his eyes dart away. "They thought it was best to wait until I left for college, which made the last two years since Grady left for school absolutely miserable because the hatred between them became so much more apparent."

"Yikes. I'm sorry, that must be tough."

"They only talk to each other through me. And if I got home late, or got a bad grade, they'd both separately lecture me about it, double the punishment, for any minor infraction. It's intolerable."

"Super shitty to put on you," I agree. How did I not pick up on all that he's been going through? He did seem to shut down when elaborating on how his family is moving, but he always kept the conversation light enough that I didn't realize there was something deeper lurking beneath.

"I don't even know why I'm mentioning it, other than the fact that one of my absolute favorite places to be is Roll Again. Especially when I get to play against you," he says, leaning closer to me as well.

I nod so many times my head might roll off. "I understand that. I love playing against you too."

"I don't know what the rest of this summer is going to look like. But absolutely everything is changing, and I've been thinking . . . that means that I want as much of it to stay the same as long as it can." He takes a deep breath. "*If* it can," he adds, withdrawing again, tangled up in thoughts I'm not privy to.

"If it can?"

"And right now it's hard not to feel like I'm also somehow causing a rift between you and your sister."

This catches me completely off guard. "What does Amelia have to do with anything?"

"You're mad at her," he says, like it's obvious.

"Sure, yeah, but we're not, like, *fighting*. This is just the same normal shit it's always been. Which has nothing to do with you?"

"But I'm not exactly helping the situation," he points out, digging in his heels, the wheels in his brain spinning way off the track. "You're mad that she left you here with *me*."

"No, I'm happy to be here with you." My expression isn't too delighted right now, however.

There's a loud noise from the arcade area, and the two girls come running out, bickering and shoving each other to get to the worker at the desk. She must be their parent or caretaker, because she shushes them and quickly plays mediator before sending them back to the games with a few more quarters.

I turn to Declan, still confused about where he's going with all this. "What exactly are you trying to say?"

"That everything's complicated, and I don't want *you* to be complicated." His eyes are wide, earnest.

Yet I respond with a fighting tone. "So now I'm complicated?"

"No, that's not—"

"Or you're saying that I'm easy?" I ask, lashing out with the opposite. "But somehow that still doesn't mean things are simple enough for you?"

He's stern again, jaw set, brow furrowed. Where is he going with all this? I miss happy-go-lucky Declan. Maybe he's the one who's too complicated, honestly; this does feel like a projection. "Iris, that's not at all what I'm saying."

"What are you saying? Because what I'm hearing is a lot of leaps. Like, I promise things always turn out fine with my sister. And you and me are good." I reach out to take hold of his hand, but he pulls away. *"Oh."*

Declan's conclusion dawns on me slowly. He's calling it quits, and I don't fully understand why.

I get that it's his choice. Yet we could've talked about it first, right? Figured it out together, like a team. But that's the whole point—he doesn't want to be a team. He doesn't have to consult me . . . to decide to end things with me.

"I'm sorry," he whispers, laying his arms on the table as though surrendering. "I don't think I'd be a good boyfriend right now."

"Hmm." I blink several times, not prepared for this at all. He's framing it like it has nothing to do with me, but that could just be him trying to let me down easy. I thought he liked me. He apparently doesn't like me enough to want to be with me. Even though this whole thing was his idea to begin with, wasn't it?

Admittedly, didn't I sort of pry it out of him? In the hot tub, when he said he had something to tell me, he immediately chickened out until I insisted that he say whatever it was he wanted to say. It's not like I forced him to tell me, though.

He didn't *have* to tell me. We didn't *have* to be in this position right now.

Either way, we're over before we ever really started.

I refuse to let Declan see me cry. I hop down from the tall barstool chair and walk toward the rental counter, my ponytail swaying in my wake.

"Where are you going?" he calls after me.

"To rent a freaking pair of skates. Because *I* want to roller-skate."

"Okay." Declan slides off the chair and takes a few steps to follow me. "It's just that I don't know how to roller-skate."

"Good thing I didn't invite you to join," I call over my shoulder.

The worker, who definitely heard the latter half of our conversation, guesses my shoe size correctly and slides them to me across the counter as I hand her the cash. I find a seat in a lower chair closer to the rink's entry and lace up my skates tightly until I might cut off the circulation in my feet, which seems impossible because of how worn out these old rentals are. But the skates do keep my ankles secure as I stand with a wobble and slowly march my way from the carpet onto the smooth wooden flooring.

I hold on to the wall for a few paces until I get the hang of things, then round the bend, going slowly, where I observe Declan sitting back at the table, not on his phone or anything, just staring down at the floor.

Maybe I should've complained about Amelia less. Maybe I should've been more attentive to asking about what was going on with his family. Or maybe this was always the inevitable outcome and I should just be glad the Band-Aid was ripped off quickly before it'd take too much of my skin along with it.

I want to be mad at him, but right now Declan seems so sad.

With my shoulder, I try to discreetly wipe away the water pooling in my eyes, but it throws me off balance, and I rush into the wall to avoid falling to the floor. It must've been a loud *thunk*, because Declan looks my way.

I hold my head high and skate around again.

And again, and again, gaining confidence with each lap, floating into a sort of meditative state as my mind replays the conversation with Declan, except with my own imagined flourishes—additional questions, or anger, or compassion—until I've altered the outcome so many times that my memory can't be certain exactly how it all went down in reality.

Chapter Seventeen

I don't leave the roller rink until I get a call from what I assume is the auto shop. I answer the unknown number, but I can't hear what's being said, so I wave to Declan and lean over the wall to pass him my phone. Then I exit and return the rental skates, Declan trailing half a foot behind me as we walk back over to the mechanic without saying a word. We hop in the car, and the GPS says it'll be a smooth, no-traffic four hours back to Omaha.

For the first half, we listen to the radio since I can't be bothered to put on a playlist. What songs would even fit this vibe? Trapped in a car with a guy who is causing me emotional whiplash, having gone from a friendly rival I had no romantic interest in to being a guy I've kissed and am developing feelings for but anything between us is over before it even really started.

Sure, Taylor Swift probably has something close, but the last thing I need right now is Declan trying to scrutinize my song choice.

It's just, like, a week ago, this entire set of circumstances would've baffled me, yet right now I'm so stuck in it that I can't see the forest for the trees.

Halfway through, we top off the gas tank and switch drivers, and Declan puts in his home address as our next stop. He breaks the silence with what he incorrectly assumes might be a neutral topic. "When would you be interested in putting together the final touches before submitting the road trip board game? We could meet at Roll Again."

He thinks we're still doing that? We did most of the work already, and there's no reason not to other than . . . I don't want to. And that's a good enough reason for me right now.

"It doesn't seem original enough, honestly."

Declan pulls away from the station and stares forward at the road, switching lanes to get us over to the highway on-ramp. "What do you mean?"

"I don't think we should finish it, actually," I say, trying to keep my voice level, which isn't hard, because I feel utterly deflated.

"We could just submit what we have and see what happens?" he says, grasping at straws.

"No, no . . . it really doesn't seem worth giving it a try anymore," I say, wondering if my double meaning is apparent. Internally, I smirk at how my point would've been much clearer if I'd used the word *complicated* in there somehow.

"I guess not," he relents.

We finish the rest of the drive in silence. I'm so tired of being on the road. If I never see another billboard again, it'll be too soon. There are so many times I half turn toward him, wanting to say something, anything, but restrain myself. This is too many hours to be sitting next to a fresh breakup.

The navigation takes us to Declan's house, which is only a few neighborhoods over from my own, probably about seven or eight minutes if I had to guess. He's lived this close to me this entire time?

He parks the car on the street in front but doesn't get out.

The garage door is halfway open, revealing two competing piles of moving boxes that seem to be dividing his parents' things. I wonder if Declan will end up putting his own stuff on both sides, or not at all, paring down everything he owns to just what he can fit in suitcases to bring to college. That is stressful.

"Hey, you're home," I say softly, not really wanting him to leave now that the time has come.

"It's not home for much longer." He delays getting out of the car, and I'm half-optimistic he'll say something about us when he turns to look at me, but all he says for parting words is "I guess I'll see you around?"

The best I can muster is "Maybe."

Declan's face scrunches up—mad at me, or himself, or everything. We both get out of the car, and he hurries up the drive as I switch over to get behind the wheel, but then he turns to add, "You're right, the road trip game was probably really boring anyway."

•••••

While the journey had four of us, I finish it as I started: at home by myself. Cyclical and almost predictable. Pass Go, collect two hundred dollars, and go around the board yet again. My parents meet me on the driveway to hug hello and inspect the car, but Amelia is still out with friends.

I drag my bag inside, leaving my sister's college stuff in the car because it's not my problem, but she better clear it out as soon as possible, because it is mine to drive now, after all. I do a quick cry in the shower and attempt to go to sleep, but somehow I'm not tired.

When Amelia gets dropped off at home late, our parents have already gone to bed, but I'm still downstairs, searching for a snack in the kitchen pantry.

"Hey, you made it!" Amelia says, cheery, stepping around me to fill a glass of water at the fridge.

"Yeah," I mutter, finishing a spoonful of peanut butter and dropping it in the sink, then adding, "No thanks to you."

She kicks off her shoes in the entryway basket and takes my words as the fight instigator they clearly are meant to be. "Are you seriously mad?"

"I don't know." But I push out the kitchen chair and sit back with my arms crossed. "What exactly constitutes *mad*?"

"I'm sorry we drove home separately." Her words reek of sarcasm, even if that's not her intent. "But did you have a good time with your boyfriend?" she asks, the question eliciting an immediate negative reaction from me. There's no one who can read me better than my sister, even without being able to fully see my face. Her tone shifts to concern. "Oh, you're upset about something else?"

Because . . . well, obviously, there's so much I'm angry about right now, no matter how I try to spin it, I don't know how I'm going to say this without it seeming super childish. "I don't know. It just seems like you're ditching me every chance you get."

"I'm not—"

"You actually are." I count each instance on my fingers. "On campus. In middle-of-nowhere Iowa. All freaking summer."

"Okay, I'm sorry we drove separately the final stretch, but you can't be mad at me for the summer program?"

"Maybe I can. Because it's really adding up, Lee."

"Iris, we can't do all the same exact things anymore." She takes a seat opposite me at the table.

Yet as soon as she sits down, I stand up. "I know. And I don't expect that. It's just—it seems to me . . ." I say, pausing to consider, like I'm trying to make some brilliant outsider observation that should change how she lives her life. Some bigger picture thought that will distill why she's trying to leave me in the dust. "That you're trying really hard to be a different person. Pretending to be someone you're not."

Amelia takes a deep breath. "Iris, it's late."

"Sure, go to bed." I cross my arms, feet planted on the ground in a fighting stance, making it apparent that I'm not going anywhere.

"Not while you're still upset. Sit back down."

"Don't tell me what to do" tumbles out of my mouth as a gut reaction, but I return to my chair.

My sister wipes her hand on her forehead and sighs. "Okay, well, how am I pretending? Other than just growing up and trying new things?"

I search for my strongest argument. "Like, not telling your new friends about your vision."

She tilts her chin, fielding the comment that must've seemed to come out of nowhere. "That's what you're being so dramatic about?"

"I don't know. I don't think *I'd* do the same. It can't be healthy for you to be hiding such a big part of who you are."

"It's a big part of *who* I am?" Amelia unpacks this. "Or is it just how I exist in the world? It doesn't have to be everything. It doesn't have to be the first thing someone new knows about me. I think I've got a pretty good handle on this whole situation." She goes in for the kill. "But you know what? If *you* get Stargardt's, then *you* can try something different."

I'm quiet.

Maybe too quiet.

Amelia is quick to walk back her words. "You probably won't. It isn't even worth talking about."

I stare down at the table, wondering if she'll even realize that I'm no longer making eye contact. "Easy for you to say."

"Easy for *me* to say?" The lines that crease across her forehead scream that I misspoke.

"I don't mean it like that. It's just . . . it's heavy."

"Okay." Her voice is still terse, but her expression has softened.

"It's hard to be calm about the likelihood of both my hearing and vision slipping away from me," I explain. "I try to think logically about it, but it's not a very *logical* thing and therefore hard to be rational about. I don't understand it. I don't want to understand, and—"

"Iris." Amelia nods multiple times, like she's going to give me some real talk that will solve this. "I mean this in the nicest possible way. Shut up."

The metaphorical equivalent of slapping me across the face. I'm pissed and gearing up to make this a *real* fight.

But then Amelia's expression softens, her voice slowing down as she pulls out the worst possible move in a spat: She goes and says something nice. "I'm sorry you're trying to process all that and feeling like I've been abandoning you." Is she starting to tear up? Shit, I didn't mean to make her cry. "I mean, you are *always* going to be in my life. And I'm sorry if sometimes I take that for granted and don't make enough time for just the two of us. Because I love spending time with you. Really. You're my favorite person in the entire world."

"Yeah . . ." I cross my arms but feel slightly appeased. "Same."

She taps her fingers on the table while she steadies herself again. "I know you already know this, but I feel like there's one other thing that needs to be said."

My stomach twists. I have no idea what this could possibly be about. "What?"

"It's just—well, just because I stopped playing Rivalry doesn't mean you would need to."

"Why would I stop playing?" I ask, not immediately putting two and two together.

"You don't need to," she repeats. "But just in case for some reason you think my diagnosis and stopping playing went hand in hand. That wasn't the reason. You could keep playing."

Something settles within me that I hadn't realized was concerned. "That's good."

"I'm sorry I dismissed the large-print version you found. That was a little snobby of me."

"Wait," I say, pulling my phone out of my pocket. "Can you say that again and record it?"

Amelia shakes her head, the way she does when I'm making a joke out of a serious conversation. "I'm only saying maybe we could try playing again together sometime. Since it's important to you. How about we do something Saturday?"

I shake my head, annoyed that she forgot about one of my biggest plans of the summer. "I'll be at the expo all day . . ."

Without missing a beat, she says, "I could come with!"

"You don't want to."

"I do! I want to see your board game creations win."

"It's not going to. And"—I don't want to say Declan's name, so I avoid doing so—"I'm only submitting the one. We gave up on the team submission."

Amelia is quiet for a moment, finally sensing that something must've happened on the way home. "Why?"

"Just 'cause."

She decides now isn't the best time to pry into the obvious situation with Declan that I'm not telling her about since we've already covered a lot tonight. "Well, I'm coming with to the expo."

"You'll have to see if there's still tickets available."

"I'll check right after this." She holds up her phone.

"They're not super cheap."

"I'll figure it out."

"You really don't have to go. I'll be busy with the gameplay tournament part too."

Amelia stands up, having conclusively decided and therefore no longer wanting to deliberate this point. "Then I'll be there to cheer you on."

"This feels a little condescending now."

"It's not." She steps over to wrap her arms around me in a hug. "I want to be there for you."

Chapter Eighteen

The Omaha Board Game Expo is at a large convention center, with different booths on the main floor and several breakout rooms where tournament matches are taking place. Amelia managed to scrounge up a basic attendee badge. Meanwhile, my badge identifies me as both a competitor and a contest entrant, so a few of the more extroverted attendees have very nicely asked about my creation while telling me about their own. The exchanges have all been lovely and friendly, but the other games sound so incredible that I doubt Craft a Witch will amount to much.

After an initial hour of exploring, I refresh the app to see if I've been assigned to my first match in the Rivalry tournament yet.

I have been assigned. "Ugh."

"What?" Amelia asks, peering over my shoulder. She's holding the clear plastic tote bag with my Fortune Teller character kit inside.

I zoom in on my phone screen and hold up the large-text name on my screen.

"Oh, you're playing Declan?" she says, confused by my reaction.

"Yeah, and I was kind of hoping to be able to avoid him today." I shake my head but start walking us toward breakout room number three, where my playing table will be.

"All right, so are you going to tell me what exactly happened there?" Amelia asks. "You two were getting along so well."

"I thought we were, too, but not well enough, I guess."

Amelia nods knowingly. "I'm sure the stuff with his parents is—"

I consult the convention center map in the hallway and discover that we have to go up the nearby flight of stairs. "How do you know about that?"

"Grady told me."

Sure, because she and Grady are still flirty friends. Glad that situation is working out for them. I'm not bitter at all.

"Right," I say, slightly out of breath after ascending to the second floor.

My sister continues to share what she learned from Declan's brother. "Grady felt bad about how much Declan had to deal with on his own these past two years."

"Yeah, it does seem tough," I admit, pushing through the double doors to the room that has a sheet of paper taped outside labeling it number three.

Though I knew he'd be there, I'm not quite ready to see Declan and Grady checking in at the front table. Declan's in his usual yellow sweatshirt, his Space Pirate box in hand, looking so familiar it hurts. I wish I could just snap my fingers and erase the entire road trip so that this could be completely normal.

But it's not like our Space Pirate or Fortunate Teller decks realize that anything between us is different.

"Hey," Declan says quietly, slipping into his chair at the table.

I nod in return, taking my place.

"I'm rooting for both of you," Grady says with a large smile, pointing enthusiastically at us with each hand.

"You know they're playing *against* each other," Amelia corrects, some of her original snark returning, but she seems happy to see him. "Is there anywhere for us to sit?"

Grady leads her over to a row of chairs along the wall, where they won't actually be able to watch any of the matches, so I suspect it'll be a fairly boring time. But Amelia insisted on coming to the expo, so ah well.

A member of the tournament staff stops by to give Declan and me the official score card. The only stat it asks for is the winner and each player's final health result.

"Less data than you're used to," I say to Declan. "You didn't bring your notebook?"

He hesitates, unpacking his box. "I didn't think it was likely that I'd be up against someone I knew."

Right, because that's all I am to him. *Just someone he knows.* I never should've expected to be anything more than that.

We roll our starting dice, and he goes first, and quickly enough we fall back into routine, but it's as if we're passively watching ourselves play. I leverage an action card, he rolls dice and hopes for the best, and repeat ad nauseam.

Sometimes I glance toward him when I feel certain I won't catch his eye, and when I focus on reading a card, I can feel his gaze watching me closely, but if I look back up, his eyes dart away. It's almost like it could be so easy to break the ice between us, but we don't know how. Or don't want to.

My heart isn't in it. I don't even care if I lose . . . which I do.

"Sorry," Declan whispers as I lower my final health status.

"It doesn't matter," I say, grabbing the pen to record our final scores on the paper. I sign my name at the bottom; Declan signs his and waves over the staff to come attest and collect our results card. Amelia and Grady are at their seats, whispering conspiratorially. I motion for my sister to meet me at the door and leave the table without saying goodbye.

•••••

Since I'm not advancing in the tournament, there's a lot of time to kill until the board game creation winners are announced, so Amelia and I explore the Artists' Alley. My sister buys a little crochet fox that she finds adorable even though it's a character in a board game she's never played.

I'm dragging my feet from booth to booth, not wanting to be here. "We might as well go home," I say.

"What? No, we have to wait for the announcements!" Amelia holds up the little fox and uses a baby voice. "We gotta see if you win!"

"Do you remember everyone we've talked to and all their much better-sounding games? I'm not going to win." There isn't much seating on the main floor, so I walk over to the wall and slide down to the ground.

Amelia points to the nearby food window. "Okay, I'm going to get us some sugar, then you'll be excited again."

She returns with fried dough covered in an excessive amount of powdered sugar that admittedly does make me feel a lot better as I scarf it down in what must be a record number of bites.

"We can get another one," she suggests.

"Nah, we don't have to."

"I'm starving; we're getting another one."

After we finish eating, content and happy and absolutely riding the sugar rush, Amelia and I find our way over to the announcement area. It's a platform stage, where there are four small circular tables with the winning games displayed under a navy sheet, to be revealed. They must also each be under some sort of box, too, unless all the winners are the exact same size, in which case, Craft a Witch is *definitely* not there, but I allow myself to maintain a smidge of optimism.

There are about fifteen rows of chairs for attendees to sit and watch the results, but I stand with Amelia along the side, not wanting to get stuck watching the team results after I lose the solo entries. That unfortunately means I notice when Declan and Grady show up and take their seats, within view of where we're standing.

A woman in her forties wearing a purple suit takes the stage with a gaggle of other somewhat eccentric but professional-looking adults. They introduce themselves and then kick things off. "Thank you all for joining us! I'm very passionate about up-and-coming board game creation, so it was such an honor to be on the selection committee. Truly, all your submissions were wonderful, and it was so difficult narrowing this down, but we're delighted to share our winners today."

She hands over the microphone to a short guy wearing a *Tetris* T-shirt. "For each category," he says, "we have an honorable mention, then a silver and a gold winner, both of which will get demo versions of their games produced by our local indie publisher, with crowdfunding established for production based on consumer demand. So, without further delay, for the individual category, our honorable mention is Cascading Atrium, submitted by Jian Zheng."

I deflate, not sure Craft a Witch could've done better than third place, and my suspicions are confirmed as silver and gold go to other competitors, neither from Roll Again, which means Declan didn't win either. I glance through the crowd and notice him. We lock eyes but immediately look away.

“Okay, well, let’s go,” I mutter to Amelia, but she shakes her head.

“We might as well hear about the team entries.”

I shake my head. “I’d rather not.”

“No, I’m curious,” Amelia says. “Please?”

“Fine.” At least I don’t have any skin in the game here.

The microphone is handed back to the purple-suit lady. “And now for our team submissions, our honorable mention is Plant Guardian, submitted by Kassie Everly and Adrianna Oktawiusz. The silver winner is Stops Along the Way, submitted by Iris Biagi and Declan Weber. Our gold winner is—” But I don’t register the rest.

Was that *my* name? My mouth hangs open while Ameila enthusiastically shakes my shoulders. “What is happening?”

Declan is walking over here. Did he somehow submit the game without me? But he doesn’t have the files.

“Did you—” Declan and I both ask at the same time, equally confused. Until our giddy, beside-themselves siblings make their secret endeavors known.

Grady holds out a thumbs-up. “You like the title we came up with?” He nods toward Amelia.

“It seemed fitting,” my sister agrees with a smile, tackling me with a hug.

“But it was . . .” I have no idea how any of this happened.

“It was mostly ready to go,” Amelia explains. “I found the files on my laptop, and Grady and I put it together. We figured we wouldn’t say anything, because if it didn’t win, no harm no foul. But—”

Grady nudges Declan and points up to the stage, where the other winners are now all gathering. "You kids got to get up there!"

"Oh," I say, but still in shock, I can't quite seem to find my way. Declan grabs my hand, and we walk together.

At the stage, we immediately separate again but are intrigued and head right up to the table where our board game creation is waiting, having been put together by our siblings. It's two laptop-sized cardboard pieces, back-to-back, with our mock-up play area pasted to the horizontal piece and a design with various different stops, including a giant mustard bottle, on the viewing area.

My favorite part is the little alien tokens that you move around to designated areas on the map. Amelia must've made these out of clay. They're grayish green with large eyes and wide mouths. They're terrifyingly adorable.

I hold one of the aliens up to Declan. "Look at this!"

He chuckles. "Better than I would've expected."

One of the judges walks by with their young kid, who is eager to stop by our board. "She loves it," the judge says, "and so do I. It's a simple round-the-board game, but with an unexpected ability to scale up the complexity. We playtested it several times and had a blast. Loved every second of it. The interplay between the cards and the dice works so well here. Congratulations."

"Thank you so much," I say as they move on to congratulate the other winners. I turn to Declan, and we share a genuine smile. I'm so excited I have no idea what to do with all these emotions. This road trip game, aptly named by our siblings, is going to be turned into an actual board game. I have to pinch myself to know this is real.

Declan opens his mouth, about to say something, but the words escape him. I don't say anything, either. Today's not about us; it's about our game.

Chapter Nineteen

On Monday morning, the day before my sister flies out to Europe, Amelia and I have breakfast with our parents, then clear the table to play Rivalry, dusting off our old Red Witch and Twilight Elf character kits. Amelia toys with her dice, clueless about how to set everything up. "I don't remember most of the rules," she warns me.

"That's okay," I say, shuffling my cards. "Easier for me to win."

She narrows her eyes, holding her magnifying app over one of her action cards, then reaching out to ask to look at one of mine. "Except my witch is infinitely more powerful than your elf." My sister finishes reading the details, then waves the card in my face. "Look at the damage this action does!"

"Only if you get the chance to use it," I tease, sitting back and letting her familiarize herself with the deck again. It's not going to be the quickest of games, but I don't mind. I'm just happy to be playing with my sister again. "Don't worry, I'm ready whenever you are."

I sit patiently as she finishes setting up her station. Out of the corner of my eye, I catch a glimpse through the kitchen window of a plane flying across the sky.

When I turn to look right at it, it disappears from my sight.

•••••

A week later, there are nearly a hundred people gathered in Peyton's backyard for her graduation party, with more arriving through the gate, a mix of classmates and family. Elizabeth and I are glued to each other's sides, following Peyton around as she makes the obligatory hellos and thank-yous to grandparents, aunts, and uncles.

I'm already nostalgic about the time left with my friends before we all scatter in our different directions for college soon.

"Wait, Iris, when exactly is your new board game going to be ready to play?" Peyton asks, stealing a few moments away from family.

"Not until the end of summer!" I call after her as her mom beckons for her to interact with a few new arrivals. I turn to Elizabeth. "We're not going to see her much today, are we?"

But Peyton turns back and points to the corner of the yard, where lots of our classmates have gathered, and says to Elizabeth, "Go ahead and tell her my surprise. I'll meet you over there in a bit!"

"Did you know she sent out a few more invites?" Elizabeth asks me.

I shake my head. "To who?"

With a sly smile, she says, "Not just people from our school . . ."

It's not hard to guess who the extra guests are. My friends have been very insistent about me getting back in touch with Declan, but I haven't known what to say, or whether it would be good for me to say anything to him at all yet. I don't want to cut him out of my life completely, but strolling back into Roll Again to play against him like nothing has happened between us doesn't feel right either.

But Elizabeth leads the way across the party to where the invited crew is hanging out. "Hey there," she says, waving hello. "All right, who's going to teach me how to play board games?" She nudges me for introductions.

"Elizabeth, this is Leslie, Shakir, Roy, and . . . Declan," I say, unable to restrain my frown as I lock eyes with him again. His shoulders are slouched, and he's almost cowering among the crowd of friends, offering a kind smile, but there's obvious panic in his eyes at what I'm going to say next. "Who I did not know would be here."

He takes a deep breath and shrugs, maintaining levity. "Turns out we both know Peyton. What are the chances?"

If the others are confused about why our interaction is so strange, they don't let on. Even though, to me, it feels like it must be painfully apparent.

"Yes," Elizabeth says, nudging me toward him, "and Peyton thought you two ought to celebrate your game creation victory."

"We've been on emails," I say, avoiding looking at Declan.

But since we don't take the hint to go somewhere else to talk about what's bothering us, everyone else clears out around us, leaving just Declan and me standing here near the bushes.

"I wouldn't have come if I knew it would bother you," he says.

"It doesn't bother me." But I'm looking back at the party trying to plot my getaway.

"How are things with your sister?" he asks.

I take a deep breath and face him. "Good. She apologized that night I got home for ditching me in Iowa. And we played Rivalry together for the first time in a very long time."

He nods. "I'm glad to hear it," he says genuinely.

It's only been less than two weeks, so I doubt much has changed with his family situation, but I ask, "What about all your packing? And your parents?"

"Still a lot. But Grady is stepping in to play mediator now, and he's much better at it than I ever was."

"That's good."

"Yeah," Declan says, not taking his eyes off me even though I keep fidgeting and looking around. "Um, Iris." He reaches out and hesitantly touches my arm, reminding me of how we held hands while walking up to the stage at the expo. Not like I could have forgotten. Except maybe it seemed like I did, because after we got off the stage, we went home and haven't seen or talked directly to each other since. "I miss you."

My stomach sinks. *No, no, no.*

I've had enough time to sit with this to realize that I can't go back to being friendly with Declan no matter how much I may want to, and if he's somehow about to ask for more, I can't be with someone who can be that cavalier and fickle with my emotions, especially not right now.

Not when everything has changed.

To be fair, no one knows except me.

I'll tell my parents, obviously, soon enough. We'll get the eye exams booked and everything that comes with that, and the diagnosis I feared was on the horizon will officially be here. Yet for now I'm going to keep this to myself. To sit with it since there's no immediate urgency. To figure out how I want this all to unfold.

When thinking about the possibility of this diagnosis, I'd usually waver between catastrophizing and considering that nothing would be any different. The reality turns out to be somewhere in the middle. Like a new pair of shoes that takes a while to get comfortable but I eventually wear every day without a second thought.

I'm just not there yet.

It's still fresh.

I wake up each morning unsure if I feel any different, but honestly, I haven't had time to figure out how I feel yet. What's the next step in life once the scary thing you worried would happen actually plays out?

Now here stands Declan—adorably wide-eyed and hopeful, seemingly eager to rekindle what we started on the road trip—and a big part of me wishes I could say yes when he asks, "Iris, do you think we could get together sometime?"

Hasn't this been lurking in the back of my mind this entire time? Haven't I been desperate to hear him ask me exactly this? Isn't my heart doing somersaults at the prospect of us being together again?

I stand on my tiptoes and plant a soft goodbye kiss on his cheek. "Now really isn't a good time."

Chapter Twenty

One Week Before Starting College

I don't go to any Rivalry nights at Roll Again all summer. Partly because I'm avoiding Declan, partly because Amelia and I have started playing the new online version as a way to keep in touch while she's in Europe. It's a lot easier for her to zoom in on the cards on the brightly lit computer screen, which makes a world of difference in how quickly we're able to play through a game.

I've also been busy with doctors' appointments, time with Peyton and Elizabeth, and a weeklong orientation session to get ready for my first college semester this fall. Admittedly, I was wondering if I'd run into Declan while on campus, but apparently, the same coincidence isn't likely to happen twice.

Except right now I'm on my way to see him, since the Stops Along the Way demo edition has finished production. We've been on the same email chain all summer, respectfully taking turns to answer the publisher's questions and signing off on various decisions, but now that it's a real, polished game, we're getting the chance to play it.

Together.

For the first time.

I get to the publisher's office first and make small talk with the staff while waiting for Declan to show up. For a brief moment, I worry he won't.

But he does.

He's wearing the green hoodie today. Back to the same Declan I've always known. I would love nothing more than to have him wrap his arms around me in a big hug hello, letting everyone in this room know that we're something to each other, even if we don't know exactly what.

He stops short of approaching me. "Hey, Iris." Hearing him say my name is enough to resurrect plenty of longing and hurt.

"Hi, Dex," I say, his nickname feeling awkward and wrong coming out of my mouth, more like it's creating a layer of distance between us rather than familiarity, and he squints with uncertainty at my use of it.

We chat with the staff and other winners until we're led to our game table, a small one in the corner where we aren't able to sit opposite but have to cozy up next to each other.

Declan runs a hand back through his hair. It's grown longer in a way that suits him. I doubt he's gotten a cut all summer. "Hey again," he says when it's just the two of us.

"Hey." I smile, though it continues to break my heart a little seeing him, especially sitting this close.

He bites his lip. "I was sort of hoping I'd run into you at orientation."

"Ah, I went to the last July one."

He nods, understanding. "I went the first week of August."

"Guess we just missed each other, then."

"Ships in the night," Declan says.

We stare down at the board game box, no longer a mess of glued cardboard, but a real, polished, and professional game. The artist the publisher hired did an amazing job designing a travel map for the cover, complete with aliens peeking in from opposite ends of the box.

"This looks great," I say as I unbox it and reveal the pieces inside. "Ooh, we get to break everything out of the perforations too. I love a fresh unboxing." I poke out a few tokens before offering the sheet to Declan. "Oh, I'm sorry. I should let you do a few if you want."

He laughs. "You look way too thrilled about doing that; I can't take it away from you."

"Thanks." I smile and pop out another token.

Declan fishes around the box for the alien meeples. They're still cute, but a little generic in their small wooden stature. "Less heart than the ones our siblings made, got to say."

"Ah, consumerism couldn't handle that level of handmade charm," I joke. "I hope I remember the rules."

He picks up the instruction sheet, pointing to a section I rewrote over email. "This part makes a lot more sense now."

"Thanks," I say. "I felt like I had to figure out all the words since you managed all the math and map coordinates."

We set up our individual boards, but Declan seems to get nervous that this might be our only chance to chat, so he asks more catching-up questions. "So, how have you been doing?"

"Good," I say, and mostly mean it. "You?"

He nods. "My parents just signed their divorce papers, to everyone's relief."

"Even I'm relieved for you," I say.

"Yeah, my mom just bought a smaller place here in town, whereas my dad's going to go move in with his brother in Boston for a little while."

"Guess you won't need an invite to Thanksgiving, then," I say, meant to be a friendly callback to one of our earlier conversations, but it does seem a little like I'm relieved to not have to make good on my offer. Which makes me decide to share my own update, though I'm nervous, so I toy with the alien meeple in my hands. "I, um, well, the thing with my eyes, yeah, that happened."

"Oh," he says, voice full of concern but not necessarily pity as he gently nudges his arm against mine. "How do you feel about that?"

"It's ongoing," I say, avoiding his gaze, but then I turn to face him with a smile. "Yet I'm still me."

He returns the smile with a knowing nod. "And it's really nice to be playing with you again."

"It is." I draw the first card from the stack and place it face up on the table between us, angling my own board so that we can't see each other's coordinates despite sitting side by side. "In a game we created, even!"

“Yeah!” He draws the next card, and our arms brush again, and this time I don’t lean away. We stay close together, huddled over our boards.

Our proximity reawakens a comfort within me. I glance up at him out of the corner of my eye and catch his gaze, feeling the warmth of his presence send my heart racing. I can practically feel the memory of his lips pressed against mine . . . along with a wild, striking certainty that it won’t be the last occurrence.

I try to hide my blush, but when I discover him matching my smile yet again, I’m positive he’s thinking the exact same thing.

Unable to stop grinning, I refocus my attention to the table—since, once again, everyone else is playing around us while Declan and I are stuck in our own little world. I move my alien three spaces to the left and pick up the sparkling blue dice.

“I’m going to start borrowing your strategy,” I tell him.

“Oh, really?”

I shake them in my hands, ready to roll onto the table. “Let’s see what these dice can do.”

Expansion

Thanksgiving Break–
Junior Year of College

It's Wednesday afternoon, and the campus parking lot has cleared out, with everyone in a rush to drive home for the holiday tomorrow. It isn't cold enough for me to be wearing a jacket, but I've been standing outside too long and the tops of my ears are frozen since my hearing aids make them stick out from my head farther than they would otherwise. Class wrapped up early this morning. I should be at least an hour or two into my journey back to Omaha right now, but instead, I'm standing here, watching this old sedan get lifted onto the ramp of the flatbed truck to be towed away for good.

My car managed to roll along for a good twelve years, yet now it's destined for the junkyard. It's given me a lot of grief, but plenty of good times too.

I video call my sister, holding the phone up so she can take in the whole scene, but Amelia answers with "Hey! What exactly am I supposed to be looking at here?"

"Say goodbye to the car," I explain.

"Oh, shit, really?" She peers forward, her nose and the edge of one eye taking up the entire screen. She isn't too surprised, however—each trip to the mechanic the last few years became a question of *Is this fix more expensive than the car is worth?* This farewell has been a long time coming, but the battery was supposed to hold out at least until the end of this school year.

But things rarely play out the way they're *supposed* to.

Life always seems to have other ideas. I'm just trying to trust that it'll get me where I need to go eventually.

"Mom and Dad didn't tell you?" I ask.

Amelia shakes her head and leans away from the camera. "No, they're out shopping right now. So how are you getting home?"

"I have no idea."

My sister flew back last weekend. She managed to arrange her schedule to have the entire week off for Thanksgiving this year, whereas I'm probably one of the last few students still stuck on campus.

Fidgeting with a loose thread on my Butler sweatshirt, I ponder out loud, "Do I try an expensive last-minute flight with a nightmare connection through O'Hare? I'd rather take the bus, but I don't know what the departure times look like."

“Eh. Well . . .” Amelia goes quiet, as if hesitant to complete the suggestion that’s already waiting on her tongue, but she doesn’t let that stop her in the end. “You could see if—”

I know exactly what she’s thinking. More specifically, *who* she’s thinking of. “No, that’d be weird.”

She’s quick to counter. “I’m sure it wouldn’t.”

How does my sister know if it would be weird or not? I roll my eyes. “We haven’t talked since, like, May at this point, so it’s not like I can text him out of nowhere?” But I phrase it more like a question than a statement, part of me wishing it felt possible to reconnect that easily. That I hadn’t let this much time slip away.

Would he even want to hear from me? There’s no way he’s thought about me as much as I’ve thought about him.

Amelia has dropped her phone on the bed as if this isn’t a video call and appears to be leaning close to her laptop screen as we chat. “You’re making this more difficult than it needs to be.”

“Welp, there it goes,” I say. There’s a loud mechanical noise as the tow truck, with our sedan all loaded up, pulls away and drives off. I ball my free hand into my sleeve, leaving the other up to hold out my phone and show the final glimpse of the vehicle that’s taken us so many places.

“Goodbye, car.” Amelia’s nose and eye peer close to the camera once again.

Is this even more bittersweet for her now that she doesn’t drive anymore? She’s reached a point in her vision loss progression where it feels safer and more comfortable not to, and at college, she's been able to get around well enough without needing to. I'm curious how this will impact her job search, like if it'll limit her to positions that she can easily access by public transit.

Speaking of which, it turns out Amelia was looking up the bus schedules for me. "The next available bus leaves at three fifteen a.m., with a transfer in Chicago . . . and again in Des Moines."

"Two transfers?"

"It'll be about nineteen hours total."

"Shit, that's more than double the time to just drive myself, and I'd miss pretty much all of Thanksgiving Day tomorrow." I scuff my heels on the pavement. "Should I rent a car? Am I old enough to rent a car? Will there even be any cars available?"

Amelia laughs at my despair, because she thinks she has an easy solution. "Please just text Declan already."

My heart skips a beat at the mention of his name. "That would seem a little desperate, wouldn't it?"

"You *are* desperate for a way to get home. That's exactly the kind of situation you're in right now."

Walking slowly, I exit the parking lot and loop around campus back toward my residence hall. "What if I just stay here and skip Thanksgiving? Mom and Dad will understand."

"Yeah, but Granny won't. You'd be hearing about it for the rest of her life."

"I could video call during dinner."

Amelia picks the phone up, so I hold the camera back at my own face. "You wouldn't be able to hear anything if we passed your call around the noisy table," she says. "Just see if Declan is even still on campus."

There aren't many people here as I swipe my card to go in the main entrance to the dormitory. It would be the path of least resistance to stay here for the long weekend. People do that. Granny will be mad, sure, but I'll see her at Christmas soon enough. Hanging here could be fun, something different. I think Priya is sticking around—wait, she's joining Jodi's family in Carmel for dinner and I . . . would rather not. Maybe I'll just hide and binge a new show and not let anyone know I'm staying on campus.

But it would really be great to get home and see my sister and my parents, as well as catch up with Peyton and Elizabeth.

"It doesn't seem like you've texted him yet," Amelia says. "Don't make me have Grady do it for you."

"As if he has time to meddle while saving the country." Grady never fails to send out election reminders, and I know he and Amelia keep in touch somewhat regularly, but surely I can find my own way home without needing to involve Declan Weber.

"Well, just making it clear that you have options," Amelia says, winding down our call.

I don't respond as I climb the stairs to my floor and let myself into my dorm. My room is bright and welcoming, as Naomi and I have collected tapestries over the last three years to cover as many of the plain cinder blocks with as much color as possible.

"All right?" Amelia asks.

"Yeah, sure, options. Okay, well, I'll catch you later, or not, we'll see!" We conclude our goodbyes and hang up.

I flop onto the thin mattress and stare at the ceiling. *Ugh.* My brain was almost entirely free from dwelling on this boy, but here I am, already spiraling again.

It's true, college has been nothing but options, to an almost overwhelming degree. Every semester when I choose my courseload, there's more classes that I want to take than can reasonably fit into my schedule—and dozens of internships to apply for, though I've got my heart set on working at the museum here in Indianapolis next summer.

And, well, options on the romantic front, too, to a less successful extent. I've dated a bit, but mostly because it felt like I should. A guy asks me out, and he's nice, and I easily brush past any initial concerns to give things a try, and yet . . . just when I finally wrap my head around things and start to get excited about the potential of the relationship, it all crumbles.

Dating is so frustrating. The highs don't seem to outweigh the lows.

The most comfortable I've felt with a guy on campus wasn't even a dating situation. It was freshman year when I spent every single day with Declan.

Inseparable. Introducing ourselves to people as a unit.

"*We're* from Omaha." "*We* designed a board game together." ". . . Um, no, *we're* not dating." "Really, we're not. *Why do you ask?*"

Initially, I relished those questions, appreciating that everyone else clearly saw what I felt, that there was something burgeoning again between me and Declan. Because it really seemed like there was. There were plenty of moments. Lingering hands. Prolonged gazes. Trailed-off comments that almost led to a relationship-status-changing question.

But what no one saw was that every time it felt like Declan and I were ready to throw ourselves back into each other's arms again, all it took was one serious look in his eyes for me to be right back at the roller rink.

Sitting on that wobbly chair, my heart sinking in my chest, and his rejection fresh all over again, cutting deeper each time it replayed in my memory until it became all I could think about around him.

At first, I thought I could push past it. That we could get back together and suddenly it would all be fine, but every time I let my brain think *Well, maybe this time* . . . I'd realize I was just setting myself up for disappointment. That I was lowering my guard and being too vulnerable with someone who shouldn't get a second chance with my affection, because should I really give anyone another opportunity to break my heart?

But Declan wasn't anyone . . .

It was an exhausting game of mental chess, a lose-lose match against my own insecurities, in which I could only confront the negatives. The fear. All the reasons why us getting back together shouldn't have been considered in the first place.

Even though I really, really wanted to.

The final nail in the coffin was the moment when a girl pulled me to the side just before spring break to ask, "Okay, then, so is Declan single?"

And I had to say, "Yeah, I think so."

Shortly after that, without really meaning to, I began to distance myself. During sophomore year, I'd forget to answer some of his texts after class. Wouldn't be free to meet up for lunch in the dining hall. And most recently, Declan stayed in Indy over this past summer while I was back home.

I knew he was busy with people here, so I didn't reach out.

Neither did he.

It was tricky to keep our friendship going when it felt like both of us were withdrawing. Though, admittedly, I was the one who vanished first.

Simply because it hurt too much.

I thought we would reconnect this fall at the start of junior year, especially at the Bulldogs Board Game Club, which has been a staple of my college experience so far. But I've been scheduled for my part-time job in the package room at the exact same time as the meetups this semester. My boss didn't give a shit when I asked if there was any flexibility in changing that. Just told me that I should hope it wouldn't conflict in the spring and that next year, with more seniority, I could have more of a say in my work schedule.

I considered letting Declan know why I wouldn't be there, but instead, I waited to see if he'd text asking where I was . . .

and, once again, he never did. That felt like a pretty clear indication of where we're at these days, and I hate it.

As I lie here now, all messed up in my resurfaced feelings, my phone buzzes with a new text, which I assume is my parents checking in on the car situation.

But alas, my sister couldn't resist interfering and must have texted his brother, and now here's Declan Weber back on my phone for the first time in a long time. At least this means he doesn't secretly hate me or anything. I never thought he did, but sometimes the thoughts can really spiral in the silence.

I tap the screen and expand with two fingers to enlarge the message so I can read it more comfortably.

Declan: Hey! You need a ride home?

My stomach plunges, but even so, I can't resist smiling like a dork at this basic message. For no good reason other than it is nice to hear from him again.

Iris: Word travels fast

Declan: In time for me to see your car towed away down Sunset

Iris: Whoa

In that case, my sister definitely messaged Grady way before she threatened that she would on our call. Because of course she did—always trying to orchestrate the plans.

Declan: So, you ready? I was going to leave like nowish

Am I all right with another road trip with Declan? That drive back from Pennsylvania feels like ages ago. Oh my gosh, I'm basically Amelia, talking about how life feels so different after going off to college, but really, who was I at eighteen? When I'd just graduated from high school?

Someone who was naive enough to think it might actually mean something if a boy kissed me.

Yet here we are, years later, and Declan is acting like this is the most casual offer in the world. That cursed Midwest nicety is just so dang friendly it can really warp the emotions sometimes. It's just a ride to Omaha. I put a hand to my forehead and take a deep breath, reminding myself that he has a girlfriend.

Iris: Yeah, thanks, give me fifteen minutes

•••••

After using the restroom and gathering my things, I wait for Declan downstairs in front of my dorm. He pulls up in an SUV I don't recognize, so he must've gotten it somewhat recently. I step toward the passenger seat, but he turns off the ignition and gets out of the car. He's matching me in a nearly identical university sweatshirt, though his is the inverse coloring—dark blue with off-white lettering—and he's quick to comment on this. "Great minds think alike."

Without waiting for me to respond, he greets me with a hug. It's not exactly awkward, but it's so brief. I would rather we hadn't hugged at all than be left here wishing he'd kept his arms around me a few moments longer.

"On the road again," he says before popping open the trunk so I can throw my bag in. He's moving fast in a way that means I can't quite get a good, focused look at him.

"Yep." I grin, maybe too wide, too forceful, too adamant that this is fine.

We get in the SUV, fasten our seat belts, and sit in silence as Declan plugs an address into the GPS. The suggested route is currently red, projecting a lot of traffic, likely due to rush hour, in addition to all the holiday inbound and outbound travel.

"Whew." He leaves his phone plugged in and puts his hands on the wheel, sitting up straight. "Seems like it'll be a while."

"Yeah." I nod, continuing to look ahead out the window. "We can trade off at the gas stations and rest stops and such."

"Sure." Declan slowly drives us past the dorm and around the circle to exit campus. "Do you have those driving glasses like your sister yet?" he asks.

I finally allow myself to glance over at him out of the corner of my eye while he's focused on the road, only now noticing the stubble on his cheeks, the confidence in his shoulders. Is he thinking about how different I look now too? I cut my hair short, above my shoulders, since seeing him last.

"No, I still don't," I say. "Because my onset of symptoms was more delayed than hers, it's continued to be a much slower progression."

I experienced a sharp drop the last couple years, but my vision has sort of leveled out to a slow and steady decline. The doctor doesn't anticipate me even needing to consider the driving glasses for another decade or so.

Declan nods in the sort of agreeable way where you don't know nearly enough about the subject at hand but want to seem supportive. "Oh, wow, I didn't realize the same thing could play out so differently."

"Neither did I."

We go through a roundabout and merge onto the highway, slow among the city's stop-and-go traffic. Declan turns toward me, and I'm ill-equipped for the direct attention. "You're still all right with everything?"

"Yeah, mostly." I fidget with my phone in my lap. "And how are things with your family?"

He lightly taps the gas to advance the car a few more feet. "My dad's getting remarried."

"Whoa, already?"

"Kind of fast, right? Like, not too fast, but still. Dad and Chelsea are trying to be all, I don't know, aboveboard with it? They had a conversation with me and Grady before getting engaged, and then also invited our mom to attend the wedding? And she is actually planning to go? It feels polite but messy, so I don't know. Like I said . . . weird."

"I can't even imagine."

"They gave me a plus-one," Declan says, glancing through the rearview mirror as he merges into the next lane.

I laugh. "To help distract you."

"I'm not sure how distracted I could be at my dad's second wedding, but I'll probably just go alone."

"Not bringing your girlfriend?" I ask before realizing this makes it pretty dang clear that I've kept tabs on him from afar. I hope my tone was more neutral than it sounded in my head.

He taps his fingers on the steering wheel. "Um, things didn't work out with Alison."

That wasn't the response I was expecting. But rather than any sort of relief, it just makes me nervous. Like I'm speeding up a mountain road with no guardrails, dangerously close to the cliff. "Sorry to hear that."

"She was great, but we sort of realized early this summer that even though we'd been going out for a little while, it didn't really seem to have a future. Like, looking forward to junior and senior year and life after college, we couldn't see each other in the picture." He gives a sheepish, self-deprecating smile. "She was actually the one to say all this first, so I guess I'm the one who got dumped, but it really clicked with how I'd been feeling, even if I hadn't realized it."

I haven't been with someone long enough to experience that numb level of detachment, to somehow reach the conclusion of a relationship in a way that feels like an inevitable path forward. "That's tough," I say, unsure what else to tell him in response because my brain is hyperfocused on the fact that he's been single all semester. Well, not necessarily. Just because he wasn't still with that girlfriend doesn't mean he hasn't dated more.

Declan's head briefly turns in my direction then back to the road as his question tumbles out of his mouth. "How about you?"

"What about me?"

He clears his throat. "Are you seeing anyone?"

A blush rises on my cheeks, but he's watching the road, seemingly unwilling to betray his own expression right now. "Long story short: I was, and then I wasn't."

"Gotcha," he says, and we both don't say anything, until he breaks the silence. "Wanna be my plus-one, then?"

I laugh. "Declan, we haven't talked for like two whole seasons, and you want me to go to your dad's wedding? I've never even met your parents."

"No better time than an uncomfortable family gathering."

"I'm sure you could find someone else to take."

"What? I know we haven't seen each other much with school and all, but we're still good friends, aren't we?" He reaches to hand me his phone. "Here, you can play Taylor Swift the entire rest of the drive."

"She's got enough songs to cover the time. We wouldn't even have to repeat any." I busy myself with changing the music, trying to ignore his ask, which is seeming more serious by the second. It's a relief that he's willing to explain our lack of interactions so easily. There really wasn't any ill intent. Life did get busy, and I needed space because he was taking up an inordinate amount of room in my mind.

Declan clears his throat. "Iris, can I ask you something potentially awkward?"

"Oh no." I chuckle nervously.

"Did you stop wanting to talk to me because I was dating someone?"

He went there. Let's clarify this real quick. "Um, no, but I did kind of assume that *you* stopped wanting to hang out with *me* because you were dating someone."

"No." Declan doesn't hesitate for even a second. "Not at all."

I take a shaky breath. "Oh. Classic miscommunication, I guess."

"You completely disappeared on me. I haven't seen or heard from you all semester." We're at a standstill in traffic, and he stares directly at me. He wants to address this seriously.

With a wince, I say, "Work schedule and . . ."

Though I can't see his face as clearly as I once did, I am without a doubt certain of the look he's giving me now. One that says *I know there's more to it than that because I know you.* One that reignites the hope I've been keeping boxed up and hidden away.

"But we were getting along so well all of freshman year. I thought maybe—"

"Okay, I'll admit that was part of the problem," I confess, unwilling or maybe unable to hear him say what I'm almost certain he was about to. "At least on my end. Distance was probably a good thing."

This time, the silence prolongs far past my comfort level. For the next hour, a full album plays through as we finally escape the city traffic to smoother sailing on the open road.

Declan nods ahead to an off-ramp. "We should fill up the tank."

We wind off the highway and to an empty station. Declan rolls down the window and talks to me from the outside as he pays for the gas. It's noisy, but when I squint and smile apologetically, he automatically knows he needs to repeat.

Declan leans against the car door and arches an eyebrow. "All right, what if we hash this out over a Rivalry match or something? Or collaborate again and develop an expansion pack for Stops Along the Way? The publisher might be interested in that since it's still selling boxes."

"I can't fully believe that people actually have our game on their shelves with other real board games."

He nods and steps to the side to put away the pump and close the tank. As he gets back into the car, he admits, "Alison asked me about it once and got a little weird when I told her that you and I had developed it together. Then, a few days later, she offered to alphabetize my game collection and basically pushed our game box all the way to the back."

I cringe that he brought up his ex again. "That doesn't seem great."

"Looking back on it, no, it really doesn't."

I never met Alison, but from the light social media stalking I definitely did when they started dating—before I limited my exposure to his posts—I gleaned that they're probably both statistics majors, so it seems likely that Declan will still have more classes with her before graduation.

Why am I feeling so jealous? Up until an hour ago, I thought they were still together, and that stirred up less jealousy in me than him talking about his former relationship now.

"Wait, did you want me to drive?" I ask before we can pull away from the station.

"Oh, sure." Declan hops out of the car, and we walk around to swap seats, our arms brushing as we cross paths.

We settle back into the SUV, and I adjust the driver's seat and mirrors. The traffic is dissipating even more, and we gained back an hour crossing into Central time, but our ETA is well after midnight.

"Another couple hours and then we can find some food?" I suggest.

"That sounds perfect."

•••••

We make small talk throughout the drive, the topic of wedding plus-ones and exes left many miles behind, and the ease of conversation makes it painfully apparent just how much Declan has been a missing piece in my life. When it's time to grab dinner, he hears my stomach grumbling and takes the next off-ramp. "We could order in the drive-through," he suggests. "But then eat in the car."

"Like in the back seat or something?" I ask, not too keen to stay stuck in the SUV, although the view through the unwashed windows of this middle-of-nowhere restaurant doesn't look particularly inviting, either. "I need a little change of scenery."

"Yeah, that sounds good."

We order, collect our food, and park beneath a streetlamp to the side of the building. Declan gets out of the car to walk around to the back while I climb over the seats to join him, having to lean forward again to grab my water bottle.

He pulls the burgers out of the bag, keeping the one without cheese for himself as he hands me the other. "Thanks," I say, unwrapping the paper and reaching for the next easy topic of conversation that I'm surprised we haven't broached yet. "How's Grady doing? He always reminds me to vote in every possible election."

Declan finishes a big bite and holds a few fries in his hand as he responds. "He's working like three different jobs at once but claims he loves it. I don't know how he's going to manage to avoid burnout, though. What about your sister?"

I shake my head. "Amelia doesn't seem sure where she wants to land next summer yet."

"There's still time until she graduates."

"Have you figured out what you want to do for work after we finish school?" I rush to eat more of my burger, because if there's food in my mouth, I can at least momentarily prevent myself from referring to me and him as a *we* again.

"I've been narrowing in on scientific research, like analyzing data in the public health field most likely."

"Interesting. I was wondering what you'd do with statistics."

He takes a sip from his drink, nodding inquisitively. "What are you hoping to do?"

“I’m planning to go right into grad school. I like to spend my time learning.”

“I could see that. What’s been your favorite class so far?”

With a smile, I use the sign language alphabet to fingerspell the letters *A, S, L.* “It’s not even in my major, but my roommate Naomi and I have been taking sign language together.”

“Oh, right, I remember that.”

“It’s been cool. Naomi has some dexterity things that make using her hands difficult sometimes, but my vision makes it a little hard for me on the receptive end, so we’re in the same boat figuring it out, which is nice. Our teacher has been helpful with showing us adaptations that make sign language more accessible.”

“That’s awesome. You two decided to room together a third year?”

“Yep, planning for all four! She’s great. We started our own mini board game nights since I couldn’t make it to club meetups this semester. What about you? Your roommate freshman year was a nightmare.”

He makes a *welp* sound, leaning back against the side door. “Oh yeah, no, that turned sour real fast.”

“The guy from last year seemed nice.” I’m struggling to remember his name, though.

“Yeah, I’m still living with Aaron now. He’s cool.”

“That’s good.” I’m trying to think of more questions to ask but don’t even need to because Declan continues hyping up Aaron.

"He's from Iowa. He kind of reminds me of you a little bit—loves to play an action card, that's for sure. Though you have more success with those moves than he does. But it's a shame we haven't all played together yet. We should definitely do that when we're back from break. He asked about you a few weeks ago."

"He did?" I furrow my brows. "About what?"

"Just, like, what you were up to since you haven't been around."

A confused smile grows across my face. "Are you trying to set me up with your roommate?"

Declan laughs, caught off guard. "No, but I mean, I guess I wouldn't be opposed if that's what it took to have you hanging around again? I mean, since you made it clear that you and me isn't something that would ever happen."

"You and me?" I repeat, the smile vanishing from my face. He dismissed the notion of us so pragmatically. "Is that something that was ever on the table?"

Declan's head drops, and he wraps up his garbage, placing it back into the fast-food bag, the burger unfinished. "Well . . . back during freshman year, I thought maybe it was just a matter of time."

I try another bite, but I can't bring myself to eat anymore, either. I scrunch it up and add it to the trash, taking a sip from my water. "I'm glad I wasn't imagining that."

He's trying to keep his tone casual. "Right, there was a vibe?"

We should stop skirting around the obvious. Hopefully, this will be easier to talk about if I keep it all in past tense. There was a chance we could've reconnected *then*. I hold my chin up, poised and assured. "Yes, there was."

Declan props one leg up on the seat, resting his arm across his knee. "It could be different now," he says, eager to immediately bring us to the present. "Like, life's different, isn't it? Pretty all right, even?"

I lean against the door opposite him, my legs crossed. "But shouldn't it be possible to stay with someone during the hard times too?"

"Maybe not at eighteen?"

Head tilted, I squint. "We're not that much older. It'd still be very easy to cut loose the second things got tricky."

"I don't know. I feel like I've changed a lot over the last few years. Living in a new place, learning all sorts of things. I think I could really show up for some—" He's about to say *someone*, avoiding directly mentioning each other like I've been trying to, but he switches to "Could really show up for *you*."

There's no mistaking what we're talking about. I falter with my words and mutter, "True, I'm not the same person I was back then."

He cracks his fingers and takes a deep breath. "What if we were just meeting right now for the first time?"

"Well, that would be different . . ." I let my words trail off, unsure how much I should reveal here.

"How would it be that different?"

I cross my arms, too, hugging them tight to my chest, balling up to make myself as small as I feel. "Because, Declan, I know you, and I trust you, but for some reason, the one thing that trust can't extend to is trusting that you wouldn't immediately break up with me again."

He considers this, running his thumb beneath his chin, his brow furrowed with concern.

I try to walk back what I've just said. "Which is putting a lot of pressure on something, you know? Like, we've never actually been in a relationship before. Maybe we'd quickly find out we're not compatible. Yet it just seems like going into something a second time brings so many more expectations and . . ." I'm unsure if I'm even making sense to myself.

Declan leans toward me eagerly.

"What?" I ask softly, already having some innate sense that he's going to say something that will put my mind at ease.

He reaches out and knocks a knuckle against my knee, sending shivers across my body. "I distinctly remember you telling me that history doesn't actually *repeat*."

Somehow this is the most reassuring thing he could possibly say to me.

I reach to take hold of his hand. "You remember that?"

"Of course." Declan interlaces his fingers with my own.

I smile but shake my head wistfully, feeling myself falling with so much momentum I can't stop it, I can only try to see if his own logic could poke holes in this. "But what if I can counter that with some statistics? I don't think it's generally successful when couples break up and then try to get back together."

He's inching even closer to me in the back seat. "But were we together long enough to be counted in that data set? Like, we didn't get to the messy parts that usually break a relationship. There aren't really bad habits or arguments to rehash. We could truly start fresh."

It would be so much simpler if life offered a clean slate.

But then again, aren't all the trials throughout the journey part of what makes living worthwhile?

The past has given me plenty to consider, and being here with Declan again, I wonder if I've built one particular roadblock too high. If maybe it's time to circumvent? But at the very least, I can't leave it unaddressed. With a nervous, pretending-to-be-more-unbothered-than-I-am chuckle, I say, "Except you did still dump me in that roller rink."

Declan squeezes my hand. "What if I learn to roller-skate? Replace the negative with a positive?"

I turn away from him and sit upright. Declan follows my actions and slides farther down the seat from me, giving space. "What are we even talking about right now?" I ask, voice level. "How did we get on this subject? You were about to set me up with your roommate."

He faces ahead toward the driver's seat, briefly bouncing his leg as he says, "And I would've been a jealous wreck, so it's a good thing we abandoned that idea."

I stare at him, somehow wanting this more than anything but feeling too scared all the same. I had no idea I would see him today. There was no way for me to have possibly anticipated this conversation, even though moments like this have occasionally played out in my imagination for the last two and a half years. "Declan."

"Iris." He turns back toward me. I focus on his blue eyes and find them pleading. "What are we even risking? A friendship that's grown apart?"

I tap my fists together several times, unsure how to broach what feels obvious. "Are you just lonely? You got out of a relationship not too long ago. I'm not here to be some backup plan."

There's not a moment's hesitation for him to say, "You're *not* a second choice."

"It seems exactly like that, though."

"I'm not going to lie and say I was pining after you the whole time I was with someone else, but the only reason I even started dating anyone was because I thought you had shut the door on the possibility of us."

"And I thought I did."

"But now?"

I briefly bury my face in my hands, muffling my voice. "Declan, I don't know if this would be a mistake."

"My brother doesn't think it would be a mistake. I don't think your sister does either."

"They really love conspiring against us." I laugh. "Or *for* us, I guess would be more accurate."

"You know what Grady said when he told me you were looking for a ride home?"

"What?" I ask.

"That me and you could give things a real chance now. That is, if you're even interested."

"I am," I finally admit. I lean against the door but leave my palms open against my legs, wondering if he'll take hold again.

"It's overwhelming spending time with you again. What if it's just nostalgia or—"

"Or we should give this a try," he says, reaching for my hand just as I hoped.

"We can roll for it," I tease.

Declan pats his pockets. "I don't have any dice on me." But he's determined to find some. He leans over into the trunk to grab his backpack, searching in the pockets until he discovers two loose dice at the bottom of his bag. "Here we go."

"Yep, there we go," I say, echoing his words, wondering if I'm really ready to leave this up to chance.

He offers the classic white dice to me. "Do you want to roll?"

"You can."

"What do we do?" he asks. "Odds or evens? Or, like, four through six?"

"Um, snake eyes," I say before considering the negative connotation of what would be considered a low roll. Declan hesitates, also because I've chosen something with less likely odds than a broader category of result options like he was suggesting would've afforded.

"Okay." His voice quivers as he holds up the dice, shaking them in his hands. "Okay?"

I nod. He tosses the dice onto the seat between us, and they bounce once. Declan is hunched forward, holding his breath, watching so intently that, in this very moment, I know I don't need to wait to see the result.

Before the dice settle on a number, I reach out and knock them into the footwell.

Declan is confused. "Wha—"

But I lean forward and interrupt him with a kiss.

One that he's excited to return, running his hands up through my hair then down my back, as I lunge forward to wrap my arms around him and crawl onto his lap. Our urgency is somehow also slow and steady, exploratory and self-possessed, not racing against a clock but appreciating every single moment of connection.

Several minutes later, I lean away to catch my breath, in awe of the smile dawning on Declan's face as he gazes up at me. "We're giving this a try?" he asks, reaching to brush a finger across my neck.

"Maybe we've found the right timing," I say, leaning in to kiss him once more, giddy as he hums in appreciation and meets me in the middle. "There's really only one way to find out."

"Wait . . ." he says, noticing something. He wraps his arms behind my back and lowers us down onto the seat so we can turn to look at the dice on the floor.

"What are they?" I ask, still unable to see them clearly.

Declan reaches to clasp the two dice between his thumb and index finger, bringing them close to our faces, displaying the pair of ones staring back up at us.

"Would you look at that," I tease. I already felt assured in my decision, but a little sign from the universe can't hurt.

Declan drops the dice again, and we cuddle together across the back seat, legs scrunched tight against the door but neither of us minding the cozy, enclosed space.

"We should probably get on the road," I whisper, not actually wanting to leave yet. The sky is dark above us, and there's still a long way home.

"We will soon." Declan doesn't move either.

That's fine with me. "Okay."

He holds me close, and I rest my hand on his chest. Our breathing steadies, falling into sync. "Let's just take a moment to appreciate that we found our way back."

To each other.

Acknowledgments

This book wouldn't exist without my agent, Kari Sutherland, who helped me circumvent every single mental roadblock I encountered, and my editor, Polo Orozco, who traversed the rocky terrain of an exceptionally messy first draft to navigate this story to its most compelling result.

To the team who filled the gas tank, rotated the tires, changed the oil, and inspected the engine (you know, all the hard work that goes into the publication and promotion of this book—car puns can only go so far): Jen Klonsky, Natalie Melius, Rye White, Misha Kydd, Rachel Skelton, Ilana Jacobs, Madeline Art, Lisa Schwartz, Nicole Rheingans, Lizzie Goodell, Christina Colangelo, Felicity Vallence, Alex Garber, Carmela Iaria, Trevor Ingerson, Venessa Carson, Summer Ogata, Judith Huerta, Kaitlin Yang, and Christina Chung.

With billboards for my fellow writers who helped me brainstorm and/or listened to me stress about the tumultuous drive this book took me on: Lindsay Milburn, Sami Ellis, Ann Zhao, Jen St. Jude, Briana Johnson, Kat Hillis, Brighton Rose, Victor Manibo, Dan Finnen, Gloria Chao, Mia P. Manansala, Miranda Sun, and Riley Redgate.

Chicago, for welcoming me home after unexpected rerouting. Taylor Swift, for riding shotgun on every playlist. Mika, the best dog, who has journeyed across this country with me more times than she can count.

All the new and old friends I've met at stops along the way.

My wonderful grandparents, cousins, aunts, and uncles.

My parents and siblings, the most important travel companions, who are also the most hilarious people I know, though that fact has never been published before, so I'm saying it here because that's probably the best way I can think to say *thank you for everything*.

And last but certainly not least, my incredible readers, including the teachers, librarians, and booksellers who help folks discover my work. I'm so lucky to write these books and so very grateful for how much you've supported my disabled love stories.